Sandra Cisne

WOMAN HOLLER

and Other St

"Cisneros is the impassioned bard of the Mexican border."

—*Boston Globe*

"The author seduces with precise, spare prose and creates unforgettable characters we want to lift off the page. She is not only a gifted writer, but an absolutely essential one."

—*The New York Times Book Review*

"[Cisneros's] feminist, Mexican-American voice is not only playful and vigorous, it's original—we haven't heard anything like it before. . . . This book should make [her] reputation as a major author."

—*Newsweek*

"One of the more original and refreshing voices to emerge on the fiction scene in recent years . . . a natural writer whose unrestrained, subtly accented, and light-as-a-feather prose distinguishes her new book."

—*San Francisco Chronicle*

"Wonderful—moving, vivid, honest and very clearly the work of an author who feels great love for the people she writes about."

—*Mirabella*

"Her triumphant, earthy shout is about life as the multifaceted women in her stories live it. . . . Cisneros's prose is the kind you can taste and feel: the dusty summers of San Antonio, the colors and sounds and flavors of life in full bloom. The voices in her stories are uniquely Chicana: The emotions they evoke are universal. . . . *Woman Hollering Creek* offers a gift to the uninitiated, the chance to taste deeply of Hispanic culture while accompanied by a knowing and generous guide."

—*Houston Chronicle*

"These stories vibrate with life, they breathe and laugh and weep and rage. Cisneros's world is . . . described with fire and love, and some just plain terrific writing. Brava Cisneros!"

—*San Diego Tribune*

"[Cisneros is] a writer who takes bold chances with a firm hand; [her] words seek the line between story and music. And, as in many Cisneros stories, we are taken across the bridge of sadness with a long ribbon of laughter gurgling like the creek. These are wise works by a writer whose poetry of language matches her most basic power of story."

—*Miami Herald*

"Cisneros is a fearless writer boldly plunging into complex characters and risky situations, and in *Women Hollering Creek* she displays a virtuoso range. Cisneros has a poet's ear and eye."

—*Elle*

"A brave author. She gives her heart to her readers like a birthday present wrapped in tears. Cisneros is the whisper that you strain to hear from the mouth of a lover."

—*Kansas City Star*

"An interwoven tapestry of visions and experiences . . . vigorous, punchy and imagistic . . . Ms. Cisneros's work merges place and mind to yield a unique vision of the Southwest."

—*Dallas Morning News*

"Cisneros challenges her reader to see life as it really is—full of unrequited passions and solitary confusions, with moments of connection real but few and far between. . . . Cisneros has a fresh voice that helps us read ourselves . . . a collection that can't be ignored."

—*Detroit Free Press*

Also by Sandra Cisneros

The House on Mango Street
My Wicked Wicked Ways (poetry)

Woman Hollering Creek

Sandra Cisneros

Woman Hollering Creek and Other Stories

VINTAGE CONTEMPORARIES
VINTAGE BOOKS
A DIVISION OF RANDOM HOUSE, INC.
NEW YORK

FIRST VINTAGE CONTEMPORARIES EDITION, MARCH 1992

Published in the United States by Vintage Books, a division of Random House, Inc., New York, and simultaneously in Canada by Random House of Canada Limited, Toronto. Originally published in hardcover by Random House, Inc., New York, in 1991.

Grateful acknowledgment is made to the following for permission to reprint previously published material:

ARTE PUBLICO PRESS: "Mexican Movies" by Sandra Cisneros was first published in the *Americas Review*, Volume 16, No. 3-4. Reprinted by permission.

TRADITION MUSIC COMPANY: Excerpt from the song "Ay Te Dejo en San Antonio" by Santiago Jimenez. Copyright © by Tradition Music Co. (BMI). Reprinted by permission.

Some of the stories in this work were originally published in *Americas Review, Grand Street, Humanizarte, Los Angeles Times Magazine, The Saguaro, Story,* and *The Village Voice Literary Supplement*.

Library of Congress Cataloging-in-Publication Data
Cisneros, Sandra.
Woman hollering creek and other stories / Sandra Cisneros.—1st Vintage contemporaries ed.
p. cm.—(Vintage contemporaries)
"Originally published in hardcover by Random House, Inc., New York, in 1991"—T.p. verso.
ISBN 0-679-73856-8
1. Mexican Americans—Fiction. 2. Mexican-American Border Region—Fiction. I. Title.
[PS3553.I78W66 1992]
813'.54—dc20 91-58002
CIP

Book design by Susan Shapiro

Manufactured in the United States of America
C98

For my mama,
Elvira Cordero Anguiano,
who gave me the fierce language.
Y para mi papá,
Alfredo Cisneros Del Moral,
quien me dió el lenguaje de la ternura.
Estos cuentitos se los dedico
con todo mi corazón.

Los Acknowledgments

Mi Querido Público,

Some of the early stories in this collection were written while I was living in the guest bedroom of my brother and *hermana*-in-law's house, Alfred Cisneros, Jr., and Julie Parrales-Cisneros. For the open-door policy, for the luxury of that room when I needed to be writer, thank you.

Gracias to my mother, *la* smart cookie, my S&L financial bailout more times than I'd like to admit.

To the National Endowment for the Arts for twice saving me in one lifetime. Thank you. Always, thank you. My life, my writing, have never been the same since.

Rubén, late or early, *una vez o siempre—gracias.*

La casita on West Eleventh Street. A borrowed blessing! Thank you, Sara Stevenson and Richard Queen, for your generosity.

Las readers *de conciencia*—Helena Viramontes, Liliana Valenzuela, Sonia Saldívar-Hull, Norma Alarcón. Song researchers—Laura Pérez *y* María Herrera-Sobek. *A todas, gracias.*

Las San Antonio girlfriends—Catherine Burst, Alba DeLeon, Sophia Healy, Joan Frederick Denton, *y la* Terry "*Mujer de Fuerza*" Ybañez. Tex-Mex text inspected by Juanita "*La Tejanita*" Luna-Lawhn. *Agradecimientos. Un beso y apretón para cada una.*

La Yugo sister—Jasna "*Caramba*" Karaula. Sister, *hvala.*

Los San Antonio *vatos*—Ito Romo, Danny Lozano, Craig Pennel, César "*Ponqui*" Martínez—*gracias, muchachos.*

My thanks to *los mero meros—El* Erroll McDonald *y la* Joni Evans *de* Random House. For fierce support and fierce faith.

Praise to *la bien bien linda* Julie Grau, my editor. *Ay*, Julie, believe me, I am eternally grateful for your unflagging *cariño*, patience, and sensitivity through the labor and delivery of this book.

Gracias a la Divina Providencia que me mandó la muy powerful *y* miraculous literary *protectora,* Susan Bergholz *la brava. Hay que hechar gritos, prender velitas, hacer* backflips. *Te abrazo con mi corazón,* Susan. *Por todo.*

Damas y caballeros, un fuerte fuerte aplauso for my most special reader, the most special friend. *El* Dennis Mathis. *Mi Ojitos.*

Virgen de Guadalupe Tonantzín, infinitas gracias. Estos cuentitos te los ofrezco a tí, a nuestra gente. A *toditos. Mil gracias.* A thousand thanks from *el corazón.*

Contents

1.

My Lucy Friend Who Smells Like Corn

También yo te quiero
y te quiero feliz.
—Cri Crí
(Francisco Gabilondo Soler)

My Lucy Friend Who Smells Like Corn

Lucy Anguiano, Texas girl who smells like corn, like Frito Bandito chips, like tortillas, something like that warm smell of *nixtamal* or bread the way her head smells when she's leaning close to you over a paper cut-out doll or on the porch when we are squatting over marbles trading this pretty crystal that leaves a blue star on your hand for that giant cat-eye with a grasshopper green spiral in the center like the juice of bugs on the windshield when you drive to the border, like the yellow blood of butterflies.

Have you ever eated dog food? I have. After crunching like ice, she opens her big mouth to prove it, only a pink tongue rolling around in there like a blind worm, and Janey looking in because she said Show me. But me I like that Lucy, corn smell hair and aqua flip-flops just like mine that we bought at the K mart for only 79 cents same time.

I'm going to sit in the sun, don't care if it's a million trillion degrees outside, so my skin can get so dark it's blue where it bends like Lucy's. Her whole family like that. Eyes like knife slits.

Lucy and her sisters. Norma, Margarita, Ofelia, Herminia, Nancy, Olivia, Cheli, *y la* Amber Sue.

Screen door with no screen. *Bang!* Little black dog biting his fur. Fat couch on the porch. Some of the windows painted blue, some pink, because her daddy got tired that day or forgot. Mama in the kitchen feeding clothes into the wringer washer and clothes rolling out all stiff and twisted and flat like paper. Lucy got her arm stuck once and had to yell Maaa! and her mama had to put the machine in reverse and then her hand rolled back, the finger black and later, her nail fell off. *But did your arm get flat like the clothes? What happened to your arm? Did they have to pump it with air?* No, only the finger, and she didn't cry neither.

Lean across the porch rail and pin the pink sock of the baby Amber Sue on top of Cheli's flowered T-shirt, and the blue jeans of *la* Ofelia over the inside seam of Olivia's blouse, over the flannel nightgown of Margarita so it don't stretch out, and then you take the work shirts of their daddy and hang them upside down like this, and this way all the clothes don't get so wrinkled and take up less space and you don't waste pins. The girls all wear each other's clothes, except Olivia, who is stingy. There ain't no boys here. Only girls and one father who is never home hardly and one mother who says *Ay! I'm real tired* and so many sisters there's no time to count them.

I'm sitting in the sun even though it's the hottest part of the day, the part that makes the streets dizzy, when the heat makes a little hat on the top of your head and bakes the dust and weed grass and sweat up good, all steamy and smelling like sweet corn.

I want to rub heads and sleep in a bed with little sisters, some at the top and some at the feets. I think it would be fun to sleep with sisters you could yell at one at a time or all together, instead of alone on the fold-out chair in the living room.

When I get home Abuelita will say *Didn't I tell you?* and I'll get it because I was supposed to wear this dress again tomorrow. But first I'm going to jump off an old pissy mattress in the Anguiano yard. I'm going to scratch your mosquito bites, Lucy, so they'll itch you, then put Mercurochrome smiley faces on them. We're going to trade shoes and wear them on our hands. We're going to walk over to Janey Ortiz's house and say *We're never ever going to be your friend again forever!* We're going to run home backwards and we're going to run home frontwards, look twice under the house where the rats hide and I'll stick one foot in there because you dared me, sky so blue and heaven inside those white clouds. I'm going to peel a scab from my knee and eat it, sneeze on the cat, give you three M & M's I've been saving for you since yesterday, comb your hair with my fingers and braid it into teeny-tiny braids real pretty. We're going to wave to a lady we don't know on the bus. Hello! I'm going to somersault on the rail of the front porch even though my *chones* show. And cut paper dolls we draw ourselves, and color in their clothes with crayons, my arm around your neck.

And when we look at each other, our arms gummy from an orange Popsicle we split, we could be sisters, right? We could be, you and me waiting for our teeths to fall and money. You laughing something into my ear that tickles, and me going Ha Ha Ha Ha. Her and me, my Lucy friend who smells like corn.

Eleven

What they don't understand about birthdays and what they never tell you is that when you're eleven, you're also ten, and nine, and eight, and seven, and six, and five, and four, and three, and two, and one. And when you wake up on your eleventh birthday you expect to feel eleven, but you don't. You open your eyes and everything's just like yesterday, only it's today. And you don't feel eleven at all. You feel like you're still ten. And you are—underneath the year that makes you eleven.

Like some days you might say something stupid, and that's the part of you that's still ten. Or maybe some days you might need to sit on your mama's lap because you're scared, and that's the part of you that's five. And maybe one day when you're all grown up maybe you will need to cry like if you're three, and that's okay. That's what I tell Mama when she's sad and needs to cry. Maybe she's feeling three.

Because the way you grow old is kind of like an onion or like the rings inside a tree trunk or like my little wooden dolls that fit one inside the other, each year inside the next one. That's how being eleven years old is.

You don't feel eleven. Not right away. It takes a few days, weeks even, sometimes even months before you say Eleven when they ask you. And you don't feel smart eleven, not until you're almost twelve. That's the way it is.

Only today I wish I didn't have only eleven years rattling inside me like pennies in a tin Band-Aid box. Today I wish I was one hundred and two instead of eleven because if I was one hundred and two I'd have known what to say when Mrs. Price put the red sweater on my desk. I would've known how to tell her it wasn't mine instead of just sitting there with that look on my face and nothing coming out of my mouth.

"Whose is this?" Mrs. Price says, and she holds the red sweater up in the air for all the class to see. "Whose? It's been sitting in the coatroom for a month."

"Not mine," says everybody. "Not me."

"It has to belong to somebody," Mrs. Price keeps saying, but nobody can remember. It's an ugly sweater with red plastic buttons and a collar and sleeves all stretched out like you could use it for a jump rope. It's maybe a thousand years old and even if it belonged to me I wouldn't say so.

Maybe because I'm skinny, maybe because she doesn't like me, that stupid Sylvia Saldívar says, "I think it belongs to Rachel." An ugly sweater like that, all raggedy and old, but Mrs. Price believes her. Mrs. Price takes the sweater and puts it right on my desk, but when I open my mouth nothing comes out.

"That's not, I don't, you're not . . . Not mine," I finally say in a little voice that was maybe me when I was four.

"Of course it's yours," Mrs. Price says. "I remember you wearing it once." Because she's older and the teacher, she's right and I'm not.

Not mine, not mine, not mine, but Mrs. Price is already turning to page thirty-two, and math problem number four. I don't know why but all of a sudden I'm feeling sick inside, like the part of me that's three wants to come out of my eyes, only I squeeze them shut tight and bite down on my teeth real hard and try to remember today I am eleven, eleven. Mama is making a cake for me for tonight, and when Papa comes home everybody will sing Happy birthday, happy birthday to you.

But when the sick feeling goes away and I open my eyes, the red sweater's still sitting there like a big red mountain. I move the red sweater to the corner of my desk with my ruler. I move my pencil and books and eraser as far from it as possible. I even move my chair a little to the right. Not mine, not mine, not mine.

In my head I'm thinking how long till lunchtime, how long till I can take the red sweater and throw it over the schoolyard fence, or leave it hanging on a parking meter, or bunch it up into a little ball and toss it in the alley. Except when math period ends Mrs. Price says loud and in front of everybody, "Now, Rachel, that's enough," because she sees I've shoved the red sweater to the tippy-tip corner of my desk and it's hanging all over the edge like a waterfall, but I don't care.

"Rachel," Mrs. Price says. She says it like she's getting mad. "You put that sweater on right now and no more nonsense."

"But it's not—"

"Now!" Mrs. Price says.

This is when I wish I wasn't eleven, because all the years inside of me—ten, nine, eight, seven, six, five, four, three, two, and one—are pushing at the back of my eyes when I put one arm through one sleeve of the sweater that smells like cottage cheese, and then the other arm through the other and stand there with my arms apart like if the sweater hurts me and it does, all itchy and full of germs that aren't even mine.

That's when everything I've been holding in since this morning, since when Mrs. Price put the sweater on my desk, finally lets go, and all of a sudden I'm crying in front of everybody. I wish I was invisible but I'm not. I'm eleven and it's my birthday today and I'm crying like I'm three in front of everybody. I put my head down on the desk and bury my face in my stupid clown-sweater arms. My face all hot and spit coming out of my mouth because I can't stop the little animal noises from coming out of me, until there aren't any more tears left in my eyes, and it's just my body shaking like when you have the hiccups, and my whole head hurts like when you drink milk too fast.

But the worst part is right before the bell rings for lunch. That stupid Phyllis Lopez, who is even dumber than Sylvia Saldívar, says she remembers the red sweater is hers! I take it off right away and give it to her, only Mrs. Price pretends like everything's okay.

Today I'm eleven. There's a cake Mama's making for tonight, and when Papa comes home from work we'll eat it. There'll be candles and presents and everybody will sing Happy birthday, happy birthday to you, Rachel, only it's too late.

I'm eleven today. I'm eleven, ten, nine, eight, seven, six, five, four, three, two, and one, but I wish I was one hundred and two. I wish I was anything but eleven, because I want today to be far away already, far away like a runaway balloon, like a tiny *o* in the sky, so tiny-tiny you have to close your eyes to see it.

Salvador Late or Early

Salvador with eyes the color of caterpillar, Salvador of the crooked hair and crooked teeth, Salvador whose name the teacher cannot remember, is a boy who is no one's friend, runs along somewhere in that vague direction where homes are the color of bad weather, lives behind a raw wood doorway, shakes the sleepy brothers awake, ties their shoes, combs their hair with water, feeds them milk and corn flakes from a tin cup in the dim dark of the morning.

Salvador, late or early, sooner or later arrives with the string of younger brothers ready. Helps his mama, who is busy with the business of the baby. Tugs the arms of Cecilio, Arturito, makes them hurry, because today, like yesterday, Arturito has dropped the cigar box of crayons, has let go the hundred little fingers of red, green, yellow, blue, and nub of black sticks that tumble and spill over and beyond the asphalt puddles until the crossing-guard lady holds back the blur of traffic for Salvador to collect them again.

Salvador inside that wrinkled shirt, inside the throat that must clear itself and apologize each time it speaks, inside that forty-pound body of boy with its geography of scars, its history of hurt, limbs stuffed with feathers and rags, in what part of the eyes, in what part of the heart, in that cage of the chest where something throbs with both fists and knows only what Salvador knows, inside that body too small to contain the hundred balloons of happiness, the single guitar of grief, is a boy like any other disappearing out the door, beside the schoolyard gate, where he has told his brothers they must wait. Collects the hands of Cecilio and Arturito, scuttles off dodging the many schoolyard colors, the elbows and wrists criss-crossing, the several shoes running. Grows small and smaller to the eye, dissolves into the bright horizon, flutters in the air before disappearing like a memory of kites.

Mexican Movies

It's the one with Pedro Armendáriz in love with his boss's wife, only she's nothing but trouble and his problem is he's just plain dumb. I like it when the man starts undressing the lady because that's when Papa gives us the quarters and sends us to the lobby, hurry, until they put their clothes back on.

In the lobby there are thick carpets, red red, which if you drag your feet will make electricity. And velvet curtains with yellow fringe like a general's shoulders. And a fat velvet rope across the stairs that means you can't go up there.

You can put a quarter in a machine in the ladies' bathroom and get a plastic tic-tac-toe or pink lipstick the color of sugar roses on birthday cakes. Or you can go out and spend it at the candy counter for a bag of *churros,* or a ham-and-cheese *torta*, or a box of jujubes. If you buy the jujubes, save the box because when you're finished you can blow through it and it sounds just like a burro, which is fun to do when the movie's on because maybe somebody will answer you with his jujube box until Papa says quit it.

I like the Pedro Infante movies best. He always sings riding a horse and wears a big sombrero and never tears the dresses off the ladies, and the ladies throw flowers from a balcony, and usually somebody dies, but not Pedro Infante because he has to sing the happy song at the end.

Because Kiki's still little, he likes to run up and down the aisles, up and down with the other kids, like little horses, the way I used to, but now it's my job to make sure he doesn't pick up the candy he finds on the floor and put it in his mouth.

Sometimes somebody's kid climbs up on the stage, and there at the bottom of the screen's a double silhouette, which makes everyone laugh. And sooner or later a baby starts crying so somebody else can yell *¡Qué saquen a ese niño!* But if it's Kiki, that means me because Papa doesn't move when he's watching a movie and Mama sits with her legs bunched beneath her like an accordion because she's afraid of rats.

Theaters smell like popcorn. We get to buy a box with a clown tossing some up in the air and catching it in his mouth with little bubbles saying NUTRITIOUS and DELICIOUS. Me and Kiki like tossing popcorn up in the air too and laughing when it misses and hits us on the head, or grabbing big bunches in our hands and squishing it into a tiny crumpled pile that fits inside our mouth, and listening to how it squeaks against our teeth, and biting the kernels at the end and spitting them out at each other like watermelon wars.

We like Mexican movies. Even if it's one with too much talking. We just roll ourselves up like a doughnut and sleep, the armrest hard against our head until Mama puts her sweater there. But then the movie ends. The lights go on. Somebody picks us up—our shoes and legs heavy and dangling like dead people—carries us in the cold to the car that smells like ashtrays. Black and white, black and white lights behind our closed eyelids, until by now we're awake but it's nice to go on pretending with our eyes shut because here's the best part. Mama and Papa lift us out of the backseat and carry us upstairs to the third-floor front where we live, take off our shoes and clothes, and cover us, so when we wake up, it's Sunday already, and we're in our beds and happy.

Barbie-Q

for Licha

Yours is the one with mean eyes and a ponytail. Striped swimsuit, stilettos, sunglasses, and gold hoop earrings. Mine is the one with bubble hair. Red swimsuit, stilettos, pearl earrings, and a wire stand. But that's all we can afford, besides one extra outfit apiece. Yours, "Red Flair," sophisticated A-line coatdress with a Jackie Kennedy pillbox hat, white gloves, handbag, and heels included. Mine, "Solo in the Spotlight," evening elegance in black glitter strapless gown with a puffy skirt at the bottom like a mermaid tail, formal-length gloves, pink chiffon scarf, and mike included. From so much dressing and undressing, the black glitter wears off where her titties stick out. This and a dress invented from an old sock when we cut holes here and here and here, the cuff rolled over for the glamorous, fancy-free, off-the-shoulder look.

Every time the same story. Your Barbie is roommates with my Barbie, and my Barbie's boyfriend comes over and your Barbie steals him, okay? Kiss kiss kiss. Then the two Barbies fight. You dumbbell! He's mine. Oh no he's not, you stinky! Only Ken's invisible, right? Because we don't have money for a stupid-looking boy doll when we'd both rather ask for a new Barbie outfit next Christmas. We have to make do with your mean-eyed Barbie and my bubblehead Barbie and our one outfit apiece not including the sock dress.

Until next Sunday when we are walking through the flea market on Maxwell Street and *there!* Lying on the street next to some tool bits, and platform shoes with the heels all squashed, and a fluorescent green wicker wastebasket, and aluminum foil, and hubcaps, and a pink shag rug, and windshield wiper blades, and dusty mason jars, and a coffee can full of rusty nails. *There!* Where? Two Mattel boxes. One with the "Career Gal" ensemble, snappy black-and-white business suit, three-quarter-length sleeve jacket with kick-pleat skirt, red sleeveless shell, gloves, pumps, and matching hat included. The other, "Sweet Dreams," dreamy pink-and-white plaid nightgown and matching robe, lace-trimmed slippers, hairbrush and hand mirror included. How much? Please, please, please, please, please, please, please, until they say okay.

On the outside you and me skipping and humming but inside we are doing loopity-loops and pirouetting. Until at the next vendor's stand, next to boxed pies, and bright orange toilet brushes, and rubber gloves, and wrench sets, and bouquets of feather flowers, and glass towel racks, and steel wool, and Alvin and the Chipmunks records, *there!* And *there!* And *there!* And *there!* and *there!* and *there!* and *there!* Bendable Legs Barbie with her new page-boy hairdo. Midge, Barbie's best friend. Ken, Barbie's boyfriend. Skipper, Barbie's little sister. Tutti and Todd, Barbie and Skipper's tiny twin sister and brother. Skipper's friends, Scooter and Ricky. Alan, Ken's buddy. And Francie, Barbie's MOD'ern cousin.

Everybody today selling toys, all of them damaged with water and smelling of smoke. Because a big toy warehouse on Halsted Street burned down yesterday—see there?—the smoke still rising and drifting across the Dan Ryan expressway. And now there is a big fire sale at Maxwell Street, today only.

So what if we didn't get our new Bendable Legs Barbie and Midge and Ken and Skipper and Tutti and Todd and Scooter and Ricky and Alan and Francie in nice clean boxes and had to buy them on Maxwell Street, all water-soaked and sooty. So what if our Barbies smell like smoke when you hold them up to your nose even after you wash and wash and wash them. And if the prettiest doll, Barbie's MOD'ern cousin Francie with real eyelashes, eyelash brush included, has a left foot that's melted a little—so? If you dress her in her new "Prom Pinks" outfit, satin splendor with matching coat, gold belt, clutch, and hair bow included, so long as you don't lift her dress, right?—who's to know.

Mericans

We're waiting for the awful grandmother who is inside dropping pesos into *la ofrenda* box before the altar to La Divina Providencia. Lighting votive candles and genuflecting. Blessing herself and kissing her thumb. Running a crystal rosary between her fingers. Mumbling, mumbling, mumbling.

There are so many prayers and promises and thanks-be-to-God to be given in the name of the husband and the sons and the only daughter who never attend mass. It doesn't matter. Like La Virgen de Guadalupe, the awful grandmother intercedes on their behalf. For the grandfather who hasn't believed in anything since the first PRI elections. For my father, El Periquín, so skinny he needs his sleep. For Auntie Light-skin, who only a few hours before was breakfasting on brain and goat tacos after dancing all night in the pink zone. For Uncle Fat-face, the blackest of the black sheep—*Always remember your Uncle Fat-face in your prayers*. And Uncle Baby—*You go for me, Mamá—God listens to you*.

The awful grandmother has been gone a long time. She disappeared behind the heavy leather outer curtain and the dusty velvet inner. We must stay near the church entrance. We must not wander over to the balloon and punch-ball vendors. We cannot spend our allowance on fried cookies or Familia Burrón comic books or those clear cone-shaped suckers that make everything look like a rainbow when you look through them. We cannot run off and have our picture taken on the wooden ponies. We must not climb the steps up the hill behind the church and chase each other through the cemetery. We have promised to stay right where the awful grandmother left us until she returns.

There are those walking to church on their knees. Some with fat rags tied around their legs and others with pillows, one to kneel on, and one to flop ahead. There are women with black shawls crossing and uncrossing themselves. There are armies of penitents carrying banners and flowered arches while musicians play tinny trumpets and tinny drums.

La Virgen de Guadalupe is waiting inside behind a plate of thick glass. There's also a gold crucifix bent crooked as a mesquite tree when someone once threw a bomb. La Virgen de Guadalupe on the main altar because she's a big miracle, the crooked crucifix on a side altar because that's a little miracle.

But we're outside in the sun. My big brother Junior hunkered against the wall with his eyes shut. My little brother Keeks running around in circles.

Maybe and most probably my little brother is imagining he's a flying feather dancer, like the ones we saw swinging high up from a pole on the Virgin's birthday. I want to be a flying feather dancer too, but when he circles past me he shouts, "I'm a B-Fifty-two bomber, you're a German," and shoots me with an invisible machine gun. I'd rather play flying feather dancers, but if I tell my brother this, he might not play with me at all.

"*Girl.* We can't play with a *girl.*" *Girl.* It's my brothers' favorite insult now instead of "sissy." "You *girl,*" they yell at each other. "You throw that ball like a *girl.*"

I've already made up my mind to be a German when Keeks swoops past again, this time yelling, "I'm Flash Gordon. You're Ming the Merciless and the Mud People." I don't mind being Ming the Merciless, but I don't like being the Mud People. Something wants to come out of the corners of my eyes, but I don't let it. Crying is what *girls* do.

I leave Keeks running around in circles—"I'm the Lone Ranger, you're Tonto." I leave Junior squatting on his ankles and go look for the awful grandmother.

Why do churches smell like the inside of an ear? Like incense and the dark and candles in blue glass? And why does holy water smell of tears? The awful grandmother makes me kneel and fold my hands. The ceiling high and everyone's prayers bumping up there like balloons.

If I stare at the eyes of the saints long enough, they move and wink at me, which makes me a sort of saint too. When I get tired of winking saints, I count the awful grandmother's mustache hairs while she prays for Uncle Old, sick from the worm, and Auntie Cuca, suffering from a life of troubles that left half her face crooked and the other half sad.

There must be a long, long list of relatives who haven't gone to church. The awful grandmother knits the names of the dead and the living into one long prayer fringed with the grandchildren born in that barbaric country with its barbarian ways.

I put my weight on one knee, then the other, and when they both grow fat as a mattress of pins, I slap them each awake. *Micaela, you may wait outside with Alfredito and Enrique.* The awful grandmother says it all in Spanish, which I understand when I'm paying attention. "What?" I say, though it's neither proper nor polite. "What?" which the awful grandmother hears as "*¿Güat?*" But she only gives me a look and shoves me toward the door.

After all that dust and dark, the light from the plaza makes me squinch my eyes like if I just came out of the movies. My brother

Keeks is drawing squiggly lines on the concrete with a wedge of glass and the heel of his shoe. My brother Junior squatting against the entrance, talking to a lady and man.

They're not from here. Ladies don't come to church dressed in pants. And everybody knows men aren't supposed to wear shorts.

"*¿Quieres chicle?*" the lady asks in a Spanish too big for her mouth.

"*Gracias.*" The lady gives him a whole handful of gum for free, little cellophane cubes of Chiclets, cinnamon and aqua and the white ones that don't taste like anything but are good for pretend buck teeth.

"*Por favor,*" says the lady. "*¿Un foto?*" pointing to her camera.

"*Sí.*"

She's so busy taking Junior's picture, she doesn't notice me and Keeks.

"Hey, Michele, Keeks. You guys want gum?"

"But you speak English!"

"Yeah," my brother says, "we're Mericans."

We're Mericans, we're Mericans, and inside the awful grandmother prays.

Tepeyac

When the sky of Tepeyac opens its first thin stars and the dark comes down in an ink of Japanese blue above the bell towers of La Basílica de Nuestra Señora, above the plaza photographers and their souvenir backdrops of La Virgen de Guadalupe, above the balloon vendors and their balloons wearing paper hats, above the red-canopied thrones of the shoeshine stands, above the wooden booths of the women frying lunch in vats of oil, above the *tlapalería* on the corner of Misterios and Cinco de Mayo, when the photographers have toted up their tripods and big box cameras, have rolled away the wooden ponies I don't know where, when the balloon men have sold all but the ugliest balloons and herded these last few home, when the shoeshine men have grown tired of squatting on their little wooden boxes, and the women frying lunch have finished packing dishes, tablecloth, pots, in the big straw basket in which they came, then Abuelito tells the boy with dusty hair, *Arturo, we are closed,* and in crooked shoes and purple elbows Arturo pulls down with a pole the corrugated metal curtains—first the one on

Misterios, then the other on Cinco de Mayo—like an eyelid over each door, before Abuelito tells him he can go.

This is when I arrive, one shoe and then the next, over the sagging door stone, worn smooth in the middle from the huaraches of those who have come for tins of glue and to have their scissors sharpened, who have asked for candles and cans of boot polish, a half-kilo sack of nails, turpentine, blue-specked spoons, paint-brushes, photographic paper, a spool of picture wire, lamp oil, and string.

Abuelito under a bald light bulb, under a ceiling dusty with flies, puffs his cigar and counts money soft and wrinkled as old Kleenex, money earned by the plaza women serving lunch on flat tin plates, by the souvenir photographers and their canvas Recuerdo de Tepeyac backdrops, by the shoeshine men sheltered beneath their fringed and canopied kingdoms, by the blessed vendors of the holy cards, rosaries, scapulars, little plastic altars, by the good sisters who live in the convent across the street, counts and recounts in a whisper and puts the money in a paper sack we carry home.

I take Abuelito's hand, fat and dimpled in the center like a valentine, and we walk past the basilica, where each Sunday the Abuela lights the candles for the soul of Abuelito. Past the very same spot where long ago Juan Diego brought down from the *cerro* the miracle that has drawn everyone, except my Abuelito, on their knees, down the avenue one block past the bright lights of the *sastrería* of Señor Guzmán who is still at work at his sewing machine, past the candy store where I buy my milk-and-raisin gelatins, past La Providencia *tortillería* where every afternoon Luz María and I are sent for the basket of lunchtime tortillas, past the house of the widow Márquez whose husband died last winter of a tumor the size of her little white fist, past La Muñeca's mother watering her famous dahlias with a pink rubber hose and a skinny string of water, to the house on La Fortuna, number 12, that has always been our house. Green iron gates that arabesque and scroll like the initials of my name, familiar whine and clang, familiar lacework of ivy growing over and between except for one small clean square for the hand of the postman whose face I have never seen, up the twenty-two steps we count out loud together—*uno, dos, tres*—to the supper of *sopa de fideo* and *carne guisada—cuatro, cinco, seis*—the glass of *café con leche—siete, ocho, nueve*—shut the door against the mad parrot voice of the Abuela—*diez, once, doce*—fall asleep as we always do, with the television mumbling—*trece, catorce, quince*—the Abuelito snoring—*dieciséis, diecisiete, dieciocho*—the grandchild, the one who will leave soon for that borrowed country—*diecinueve, veinte, veintiuno*—the one he will not remember, the one he is least familiar with—*veintidós, veintitrés, veinticuatro*—years later when the house on La Fortuna, number 12, is sold, when the *tlapalería*, corner of Misterios and Cinco de Mayo, changes owners, when the courtyard gate of arabesques and scrolls is taken off its hinges and replaced with a corrugated sheet metal door instead, when the widow Márquez and La Muñeca's mother move away, when Abuelito falls asleep one last time—*Veinticinco, veintiséis, veintisiete*—years afterward when I return to the shop on the corner of Misterios and Cinco de Mayo, repainted and redone as a pharmacy, to the basilica that is crumbling and closed, to the plaza photographers, the balloon vendors and shoeshine thrones, the women whose faces I do not recognize serving lunch in the wooden booths, to the house on La Fortuna, number 12, smaller and darker than when we lived there, with the rooms boarded shut and rented to strangers, the street suddenly dizzy with automobiles and diesel fumes, the house fronts scuffed and the gardens frayed, the children who played kickball all grown and moved away.

Who would've guessed, after all this time, it is me who will remember when everything else is forgotten, you who took with you to your stone bed something irretrievable, without a name.

II.

One Holy Night

Me importas tú, y tú, y tú
y nadie más que tú
—"Piel Canela"
interpretada por María Victoria
(Boby Capó, *autor*)

One Holy Night

About the truth, if you give it to a person, then he has power over you. And if someone gives it to you, then they have made themselves your slave. It is a strong magic. You can never take it back.

—Chaq Uxmal Paloquín

He said his name was Chaq. Chaq Uxmal Paloquín. That's what he told me. He was of an ancient line of Mayan kings. Here, he said, making a map with the heel of his boot, this is where I come from, the Yucatán, the ancient cities. This is what Boy Baby said.

It's been eighteen weeks since Abuelita chased him away with the broom, and what I'm telling you I never told nobody, except Rachel and Lourdes, who know everything. He said he would love me like a revolution, like a religion. Abuelita burned the pushcart and sent me here, miles from home, in this town of dust, with one wrinkled witch woman who rubs my belly with jade, and sixteen nosy cousins.

I don't know how many girls have gone bad from selling cu-

cumbers. I know I'm not the first. My mother took the crooked walk too, I'm told, and I'm sure my Abuelita has her own story, but it's not my place to ask.

Abuelita says it's Uncle Lalo's fault because he's the man of the family and if he had come home on time like he was supposed to and worked the pushcart on the days he was told to and watched over his goddaughter, who is too foolish to look after herself, nothing would've happened, and I wouldn't have to be sent to Mexico. But Uncle Lalo says if they had never left Mexico in the first place, shame enough would have kept a girl from doing devil things.

I'm not saying I'm not bad. I'm not saying I'm special. But I'm not like the Allport Street girls, who stand in doorways and go with men into alleys.

All I know is I didn't want it like that. Not against the bricks or hunkering in somebody's car. I wanted it come undone like gold thread, like a tent full of birds. The way it's supposed to be, the way I knew it would be when I met Boy Baby.

But you must know, I was no girl back then. And Boy Baby was no boy. Chaq Uxmal Paloquín. Boy Baby was a man. When I asked him how old he was he said he didn't know. The past and the future are the same thing. So he seemed boy and baby and man all at once, and the way he looked at me, how do I explain?

I'd park the pushcart in front of the Jewel food store Saturdays. He bought a mango on a stick the first time. Paid for it with a new twenty. Next Saturday he was back. Two mangoes, lime juice, and chili powder, keep the change. The third Saturday he asked for a cucumber spear and ate it slow. I didn't see him after that till the day he brought me Kool-Aid in a plastic cup. Then I knew what I felt for him.

Maybe you wouldn't like him. To you he might be a bum. Maybe he looked it. Maybe. He had broken thumbs and burnt fingers. He had thick greasy fingernails he never cut and dusty hair. And all his bones were strong ones like a man's. I waited every Saturday in my same blue dress. I sold all the mango and cucumber, and then Boy Baby would come finally.

What I knew of Chaq was only what he told me, because nobody seemed to know where he came from. Only that he could speak a strange language that no one could understand, said his name translated into boy, or boy-child, and so it was the street people nicknamed him Boy Baby.

I never asked about his past. He said it was all the same and didn't matter, past and the future all the same to his people. But the truth has a strange way of following you, of coming up to you and making you listen to what it has to say.

Night time. Boy Baby brushes my hair and talks to me in his strange language because I like to hear it. What I like to hear him tell is how he is Chaq, Chaq of the people of the sun, Chaq of the temples, and what he says sounds sometimes like broken clay, and at other times like hollow sticks, or like the swish of old feathers crumbling into dust.

He lived behind Esparza & Sons Auto Repair in a little room that used to be a closet—pink plastic curtains on a narrow window, a dirty cot covered with newspapers, and a cardboard box filled with socks and rusty tools. It was there, under one bald bulb, in the back room of the Esparza garage, in the single room with pink curtains, that he showed me the guns—twenty-four in all. Rifles and pistols, one rusty musket, a machine gun, and several tiny weapons with mother-of-pearl handles that looked like toys. So you'll see who I am, he said, laying them all out on the bed of newspapers. So you'll understand. But I didn't want to know.

The stars foretell everything, he said. My birth. My son's. The boy-child who will bring back the grandeur of my people from those who have broken the arrows, from those who have pushed the ancient stones off their pedestals.

Then he told how he had prayed in the Temple of the Magician years ago as a child when his father had made him promise to bring back the ancient ways. Boy Baby had cried in the temple dark that only the bats made holy. Boy Baby who was man and child among the great and dusty guns lay down on the newspaper bed and wept for a thousand years. When I touched him, he looked at me with the sadness of stone.

You must not tell anyone what I am going to do, he said. And what I remember next is how the moon, the pale moon with its one yellow eye, the moon of Tikal, and Tulum, and Chichén, stared through the pink plastic curtains. Then something inside bit me, and I gave out a cry as if the other, the one I wouldn't be anymore, leapt out.

So I was initiated beneath an ancient sky by a great and mighty heir—Chaq Uxmal Paloquín. I, Ixchel, his queen.

The truth is, it wasn't a big deal. It wasn't any deal at all. I put my bloody panties inside my T-shirt and ran home hugging myself. I thought about a lot of things on the way home. I thought about all the world and how suddenly I became a part of history and wondered if everyone on the street, the sewing machine lady and the *panadería* saleswomen and the woman with two kids sitting on the bus bench didn't all know. *Did I look any different? Could they tell?* We were all the same somehow, laughing behind our hands, waiting the way all women wait, and when we find out, we wonder why the world and a million years made such a big deal over nothing.

I know I was supposed to feel ashamed, but I wasn't ashamed. I wanted to stand on top of the highest building, the top-top floor, and yell, *I know*.

Then I understood why Abuelita didn't let me sleep over at Lourdes's house full of too many brothers, and why the Roman girl in the movies always runs away from the soldier, and what happens when the scenes in love stories begin to fade, and why brides blush, and how it is that sex isn't simply a box you check *M* or *F* on in the test we get at school.

I was wise. The corner girls were still jumping into their stupid little hopscotch squares. I laughed inside and climbed the wooden stairs two by two to the second floor rear where me and Abuelita and Uncle Lalo live. I was still laughing when I opened the door and Abuelita asked, Where's the pushcart?

And then I didn't know what to do.

It's a good thing we live in a bad neighborhood. There are always plenty of bums to blame for your sins. If it didn't happen the way I told it, it really could've. We looked and looked all over for the kids who stole my pushcart. The story wasn't the best, but since I had to make it up right then and there with Abuelita staring a hole through my heart, it wasn't too bad.

For two weeks I had to stay home. Abuelita was afraid the street kids who had stolen the cart would be after me again. Then I thought I might go over to the Esparza garage and take the pushcart out and leave it in some alley for the police to find, but I was never allowed to leave the house alone. Bit by bit the truth started to seep out like a dangerous gasoline.

First the nosy woman who lives upstairs from the laundromat told my Abuelita she thought something was fishy, the pushcart wheeled into Esparza & Sons every Saturday after dark, how a man, the same dark Indian one, the one who never talks to anybody, walked with me when the sun went down and pushed the cart into the garage, that one there, and yes we went inside, there where the fat lady named Concha, whose hair is dyed a hard black, pointed a fat finger.

I prayed that we would not meet Boy Baby, and since the gods listen and are mostly good, Esparza said yes, a man like that had lived there but was gone, had packed a few things and left the pushcart in a corner to pay for his last week's rent.

We had to pay $20 before he would give us our pushcart back. Then Abuelita made me tell the real story of how the cart had disappeared, all of which I told this time, except for that one night, which I would have to tell anyway, weeks later, when I prayed for the moon of my cycle to come back, but it would not.

When Abuelita found out I was going to *dar a luz,* she cried until her eyes were little, and blamed Uncle Lalo, and Uncle Lalo blamed this country, and Abuelita blamed the infamy of men. That is when she burned the cucumber pushcart and called me a *sinvergüenza* because I *am* without shame.

Then I cried too—Boy Baby was lost from me—until my head was hot with headaches and I fell asleep. When I woke up, the cucumber pushcart was dust and Abuelita was sprinkling holy water on my head.

Abuelita woke up early every day and went to the Esparza garage to see if news about that *demonio* had been found, had Chaq Uxmal Paloquín sent any letters, any, and when the other mechanics heard that name they laughed, and asked if we had made it up, that we could have some letters that had come for Boy Baby, no forwarding address, since he had gone in such a hurry.

There were three. The first, addressed "Occupant," demanded immediate payment for a four-month-old electric bill. The second was one I recognized right away—a brown envelope fat with cake-mix coupons and fabric-softener samples—because we'd gotten one just like it. The third was addressed in a spidery Spanish to a Señor C. Cruz, on paper so thin you could read it unopened by the light of the sky. The return address a convent in Tampico.

This was to whom my Abuelita wrote in hopes of finding the man who could correct my ruined life, to ask if the good nuns might know the whereabouts of a certain Boy Baby—and if they were hiding him it would be of no use because God's eyes see through all souls.

We heard nothing for a long time. Abuelita took me out of school when my uniform got tight around the belly and said it was a shame I wouldn't be able to graduate with the other eighth graders.

Except for Lourdes and Rachel, my grandma and Uncle Lalo, nobody knew about my past. I would sleep in the big bed I share with Abuelita same as always. I could hear Abuelita and Uncle Lalo talking in low voices in the kitchen as if they were praying the rosary, how they were going to send me to Mexico, to San Dionisio de Tlaltepango, where I have cousins and where I was conceived and would've been born had my grandma not thought it wise to send my mother here to the United States so that neighbors in San Dionisio de Tlaltepango wouldn't ask why her belly was suddenly big.

I was happy. I liked staying home. Abuelita was teaching me to crochet the way she had learned in Mexico. And just when I had mastered the tricky rosette stitch, the letter came from the convent which gave the truth about Boy Baby—however much we didn't want to hear.

He was born on a street with no name in a town called Miseria. His father, Eusebio, is a knife sharpener. His mother, Refugia, stacks apricots into pyramids and sells them on a cloth in the market. There are brothers. Sisters too of which I know little. The youngest, a Carmelite, writes me all this and prays for my soul, which is why I know it's all true.

Boy Baby is thirty-seven years old. His name is Chato which means fat-face. There is no Mayan blood.

I don't think they understand how it is to be a girl. I don't think they know how it is to have to wait your whole life. I count the months for the baby to be born, and it's like a ring of water inside me reaching out and out until one day it will tear from me with its own teeth.

Already I can feel the animal inside me stirring in his own uneven sleep. The witch woman says it's the dreams of weasels that make my child sleep the way he sleeps. She makes me eat white bread blessed by the priest, but I know it's the ghost of him inside me that circles and circles, and will not let me rest.

Abuelita said they sent me here just in time, because a little later Boy Baby came back to our house looking for me, and she had to chase him away with the broom. The next thing we hear, he's in the newspaper clippings his sister sends. A picture of him looking very much like stone, police hooked on either arm . . . *on the road to* Las Grutas de Xtacumbilxuna, *the Caves of the Hidden Girl . . . eleven female bodies . . . the last seven years . . .*

Then I couldn't read but only stare at the little black-and-white dots that make up the face I am in love with.

All my girl cousins here either don't talk to me, or those who do, ask questions they're too young to know *not* to ask. What they want to know really is how it is to have a man, because they're too ashamed to ask their married sisters.

They don't know what it is to lay so still until his sleep breathing is heavy, for the eyes in the dim dark to look and look without worry at the man-bones and the neck, the man-wrist and man-jaw thick and strong, all the salty dips and hollows, the stiff hair of the brow and sour swirl of sideburns, to lick the fat earlobes that taste of smoke, and stare at how perfect is a man.

I tell them, "It's a bad joke. When you find out you'll be sorry."

I'm going to have five children. Five. Two girls. Two boys. And one baby.

The girls will be called Lisette and Maritza. The boys I'll name Pablo and Sandro.

And my baby. My baby will be named Alegre, because life will always be hard.

Rachel says that love is like a big black piano being pushed off the top of a three-story building and you're waiting on the bottom to catch it. But Lourdes says it's not that way at all. It's like a top, like all the colors in the world are spinning so fast they're not colors anymore and all that's left is a white hum.

There was a man, a crazy who lived upstairs from us when we lived on South Loomis. He couldn't talk, just walked around all day with this harmonica in his mouth. Didn't play it. Just sort of breathed through it, all day long, wheezing, in and out, in and out.

This is how it is with me. Love I mean.

My Tocaya

Have you seen this girl? You must've seen her in the papers. Or then again at Father & Son's Taco Palace No. 2 on Nogalitos. Patricia Bernadette Benavídez, my *tocaya,* five feet, 115 pounds, thirteen years old.

Not that we were friends or anything like that. Sure we talked. But that was before she died and came back from the dead. Maybe you read about it or saw her on TV. She was on all the news channels. They interviewed anyone who knew her. Even the p.e. teacher who *had* to say nice things—*She was full of energy, a good kid, sweet.* Sweet as could be, considering she was a freak. Now why didn't anyone ask me?

Patricia Benavídez. The "son" half of Father & Son's Taco Palace No. 2 even before the son quit. That's how this Trish inherited the paper hat and white apron after school and every weekend, bored, a little sad, behind the high counters where customers ate standing up like horses.

That wasn't enough to make me feel sorry for her, though, even if her father *was* mean. But who could blame him? A girl who wore rhinestone earrings and glitter high heels to school was destined for trouble that nobody—not God or correctional institutions—could mend.

I think she got double promoted somewhere and that's how come she wound up in high school before she had any business being here. Yeah, kids like that always try too hard to fit in. Take this *tocaya*—same name as me, right? But does she call herself *la* Patee, or Patty, or something normal? No, she's gotta be different. Says her name's "Tri-ish." Invented herself a phony English accent too, all breathless and sexy like a British Marilyn Monroe. Real goofy. I mean, whoever heard of a Mexican with a British accent? Know what I mean? The girl had problems.

But if you caught her alone, and said, *Pa-trrri-see-ah*—I always made sure I said it in Spanish—*Pa-trrri-see-ah, cut the bull crap and be for real.* If you caught her without an audience, I guess she was all right.

That's how I managed to put up with her when I knew her, just before she ran away. Disappeared from a life sentence at that taco house. Got tired of coming home stinking of crispy tacos. Well, no wonder she left. I wouldn't want to stink of crispy tacos neither.

Who knows what she had to put up with. Maybe her father beat her. He beat the brother, I know that. Or at least they beat each other. It was one of those fist fights that finally did it—drove the boy off forever, though probably he was sick of stinking of tacos too. That's what I'm thinking.

Then a few weeks after the brother was gone, this *tocaya* of mine had her picture in all the papers, just like the kids on milk cartons:

HAVE YOU SEEN THIS GIRL?

Patricia Bernadette Benavídez, 13, has been missing since Tuesday, Nov. 11, and her family is extremely worried. The girl, who is a student at Our Lady of Sorrows High School, is believed to be a runaway and was last seen on her way to school in the vicinity of Dolorosa and Soledad. Patricia is 5′, 115 lbs., and was wearing a jean jacket, blue plaid uniform skirt, white blouse, and high heels [*glitter probably*] when she disappeared. Her mother, Delfina Benavídez, has this message: "Honey, call Mommy y te quiero mucho."

Some people.

What did I care Benavídez disappeared? Wouldn't've. If it wasn't for Max Lucas Luna Luna, senior, Holy Cross, our brother school. They sometimes did exchanges with us. Teasers is what they were. Sex Rap Crap is what we called it, only the sisters called them different—Youth Exchanges. Like where they'd invite some of the guys from Holy Cross over here for Theology, and some of us girls from Sorrows would go over there. And we'd pretend like we were real interested in the issue "The Blessed Virgin: Role Model for Today's Young Woman," "Petting: Too Far, Too Fast, Too Late," "Heavy Metal and the Devil." Shit like that.

Not every day. Just once in a while as kind of an experiment. Catholic school was afraid of putting us all together too much, on account of hormones. That's what Sister Virginella said. If you can't conduct yourselves like proper young ladies when our guests arrive, we'll have to suspend our Youth Exchanges indefinitely. No whistling, grabbing, or stomping in the future, *is that clear?!!!*

Alls I know is he's got these little hips like the same size since he was twelve probably. Little waist and little ass wrapped up neat and sweet like a Hershey bar. Damn! That's what I remember.

Turns out Max Lucas Luna Luna lives next door to the freak. I mean, I never even bothered talking to Patricia Benavídez before, even though we were in the same section of General Business. But she comes up to me one day in the cafeteria when I'm waiting for my french fries and goes:

"Hey, *tocaya,* I know someone who's got the hots for you."

"Yeah, right," I says, trying to blow her off. I don't want to be seen talking to no flake.

"You know a guy named Luna from Holy Cross, the one who came over for that Theology exchange, the cute one with the ponytail?"

"So's?"

"Well, he and my brother Ralphie are tight, and he told Ralphie not to tell nobody but he thinks Patricia Chávez is real fine."

"You lie, girl."

"Swear to God. If you don't believe me, call my brother Ralphie."

Shit! That was enough to make me Trish Benavídez's best girlfriend for life, I swear. After that, I *always* made sure I got to General Business class early. Usually she'd have something to tell me, and if she didn't, I made sure to give her something to pass on to Max Lucas Luna Luna. But it was painful slow on account of this girl worked so much and didn't have no social life to speak of.

That's how this Patricia Bernadette got to be our messenger of luh-uv for a while, even though me and Max Lucas Luna Luna hadn't gotten beyond the I-like-you/Do-you-like-me stage. Hadn't so much as seen each other since the rap crap, but I was working on it.

I knew they lived somewhere in the Monte Vista area. So I'd ride my bike up and down streets—Magnolia, Mulberry, Huisache, Mistletoe—wondering if I was hot or cold. Just knowing Max Lucas Luna Luna might appear was enough to make my blood laugh.

The week I start dropping in at Father & Son's Taco Palace No. 2, is when she decides to skip. First we get an announcement over the intercom from Sister Virginella. *I am sorry to have to announce one of our youngest and dearest students has strayed from home. Let us keep her in our hearts and in our prayers until her safe return.* That's when she first got her picture in the paper with her ma's weepy message.

Personally it was no grief or relief to me she escaped so clean.

That's for sure. But as it happened, she owed me. Bad enough she skips and has the whole school talking. At least *then* I had hope she'd make good on her promise to hook me up with Max Lucas Luna Luna. But just when I could say her name again without spitting, she goes and dies. Some kids playing in a drain ditch find a body, and yeah, it's her. When the TV cameras arrive at our school, there go all them drama hot shits howling real tears, even the ones that didn't know her. Sick.

Well, I couldn't help but feel bad for the dip once she's dead, right? I mean, after I got over being mad. Until she rose from the dead three days later.

After they've featured her ma crying into a wrinkled handkerchief and her dad saying, "She was my little princess," and the student body using money from our Padre Island field-trip fund to buy a bouquet of white gladiolus with a banner that reads VIRGENCITA, CUÍDALA, and the whole damn school having to go to a high mass in her honor, my *tocaya* outdoes herself. Shows up at the downtown police station and says, I ain't dead.

Can you believe it? Her parents had identified the body in the morgue and everything. "I guess we were too upset to examine the body properly." Ha!

I never did get to meet Max Lucas Luna Luna, and who cares, right? All I'm saying is she couldn't even die right. But whose famous face is on the front page of the *San Antonio Light*, the *San Antonio Express News, and* the *Southside Reporter*? Girl, I'm telling you.

III.

There Was a Man, There Was a Woman

Me estoy muriendo
y tú, como si nada . . .
—"Puñalada Trapera"
interpretada por Lola Beltrán
(Tomás Méndez Sosa, *autor*)

Woman Hollering Creek

The day Don Serafín gave Juan Pedro Martínez Sánchez permission to take Cleófilas Enriqueta DeLeón Hernández as his bride, across her father's threshold, over several miles of dirt road and several miles of paved, over one border and beyond to a town *en el otro lado*—on the other side—already did he divine the morning his daughter would raise her hand over her eyes, look south, and dream of returning to the chores that never ended, six good-for-nothing brothers, and one old man's complaints.

He had said, after all, in the hubbub of parting: I am your father, I will never abandon you. He *had* said that, hadn't he, when he hugged and then let her go. But at the moment Cleófilas was busy looking for Chela, her maid of honor, to fulfill their bouquet conspiracy. She would not remember her father's parting words until later. *I am your father, I will never abandon you.*

Only now as a mother did she remember. Now, when she and Juan Pedrito sat by the creek's edge. How when a man and a woman love each other, sometimes that love sours. But a parent's love for a child, a child's for its parents, is another thing entirely.

This is what Cleófilas thought evenings when Juan Pedro did not come home, and she lay on her side of the bed listening to the hollow roar of the interstate, a distant dog barking, the pecan trees rustling like ladies in stiff petticoats—*shh-shh-shh, shh-shh-shh*—soothing her to sleep.

In the town where she grew up, there isn't very much to do except accompany the aunts and godmothers to the house of one or the other to play cards. Or walk to the cinema to see this week's film again, speckled and with one hair quivering annoyingly on the screen. Or to the center of town to order a milk shake that will appear in a day and a half as a pimple on her backside. Or to the girlfriend's house to watch the latest *telenovela* episode and try to copy the way the women comb their hair, wear their makeup.

But what Cleófilas has been waiting for, has been whispering and sighing and giggling for, has been anticipating since she was old enough to lean against the window displays of gauze and butterflies and lace, is passion. Not the kind on the cover of the *¡Alarma!* magazines, mind you, where the lover is photographed with the bloody fork she used to salvage her good name. But passion in its purest crystalline essence. The kind the books and songs and *telenovelas* describe when one finds, finally, the great love of one's life, and does whatever one can, must do, at whatever the cost.

Tú o Nadie. "You or No One." The title of the current favorite *telenovela.* The beautiful Lucía Méndez having to put up with all kinds of hardships of the heart, separation and betrayal, and loving, always loving no matter what, because *that* is the most important thing, and did you see Lucía Méndez on the Bayer aspirin commercials—wasn't she lovely? Does she dye her hair do you think? Cleófilas is going to go to the *farmacía* and buy a hair rinse; her girlfriend Chela will apply it—it's not that difficult at all.

Because you didn't watch last night's episode when Lucía confessed she loved him more than anyone in her life. In her life! And she sings the song "You or No One" in the beginning and end of the show. *Tú o Nadie*. Somehow one ought to live one's life like that, don't you think? You or no one. Because to suffer for love is good. The pain all sweet somehow. In the end.

Seguín. She had liked the sound of it. Far away and lovely. Not like *Monclova. Coahuila*. Ugly.

Seguín, Tejas. A nice sterling ring to it. The tinkle of money. She would get to wear outfits like the women on the *tele*, like Lucía Méndez. And have a lovely house, and wouldn't Chela be jealous.

And yes, they will drive all the way to Laredo to get her wedding dress. That's what they say. Because Juan Pedro wants to get married right away, without a long engagement since he can't take off too much time from work. He has a very important position in Seguin with, with . . . a beer company, I think. Or was it tires? Yes, he has to be back. So they will get married in the spring when he can take off work, and then they will drive off in his new pickup—did you see it?—to their new home in Seguin. Well, not exactly new, but they're going to repaint the house. You know newlyweds. New paint and new furniture. Why not? He can afford it. And later on add maybe a room or two for the children. May they be blessed with many.

Well, you'll see. Cleófilas has always been so good with her sewing machine. A little *rrrr, rrrr, rrrr* of the machine and *¡zas!* Miracles. She's always been so clever, that girl. Poor thing. And without even a mama to advise her on things like her wedding night. Well, may God help her. What with a father with a head like a burro, and those six clumsy brothers. Well, what do you think! Yes, I'm going to the wedding. Of course! The dress I want to wear just needs to be altered a teensy bit to bring it up to date. See, I saw a new style last night that I thought would suit me. Did you watch last night's episode of *The Rich Also Cry*? Well, did you notice the dress the mother was wearing?

La Gritona. Such a funny name for such a lovely *arroyo*. But that's what they called the creek that ran behind the house. Though no one could say whether the woman had hollered from anger or pain. The natives only knew the *arroyo* one crossed on the way to San Antonio, and then once again on the way back, was called Woman Hollering, a name no one from these parts questioned, little less understood. *Pues, allá de los indios, quién sabe*—who knows, the townspeople shrugged, because it was of no concern to their lives how this trickle of water received its curious name.

"What do you want to know for?" Trini the laundromat attendant asked in the same gruff Spanish she always used whenever she gave Cleófilas change or yelled at her for something. First for putting too much soap in the machines. Later, for sitting on a washer. And still later, after Juan Pedrito was born, for not understanding that in this country you cannot let your baby walk around with no diaper and his pee-pee hanging out, it wasn't nice, *¿entiendes? Pues.*

How could Cleófilas explain to a woman like this why the name Woman Hollering fascinated her. Well, there was no sense talking to Trini.

On the other hand there were the neighbor ladies, one on either side of the house they rented near the *arroyo*. The woman Soledad on the left, the woman Dolores on the right.

The neighbor lady Soledad liked to call herself a widow, though how she came to be one was a mystery. Her husband had either died, or run away with an ice-house floozie, or simply gone out for cigarettes one afternoon and never came back. It was hard to say which since Soledad, as a rule, didn't mention him.

In the other house lived *la señora* Dolores, kind and very sweet, but her house smelled too much of incense and candles from the altars that burned continuously in memory of two sons who had died in the last war and one husband who had died shortly after from grief. The neighbor lady Dolores divided her time between the memory of these men and her garden, famous for its sunflowers—so tall they had to be supported with broom handles and old boards; red red cockscombs, fringed and bleeding a thick menstrual color; and, especially, roses whose sad scent reminded Cleófilas of the dead. Each Sunday *la señora* Dolores clipped the most beautiful of these flowers and arranged them on three modest headstones at the Seguin cemetery.

The neighbor ladies, Soledad, Dolores, they might've known once the name of the *arroyo* before it turned English but they did not know now. They were too busy remembering the men who had left through either choice or circumstance and would never come back.

Pain or rage, Cleófilas wondered when she drove over the bridge the first time as a newlywed and Juan Pedro had pointed it out. *La Gritona*, he had said, and she had laughed. Such a funny name for a creek so pretty and full of happily ever after.

The first time she had been so surprised she didn't cry out or try to defend herself. She had always said she would strike back if a man, any man, were to strike her.

But when the moment came, and he slapped her once, and then again, and again; until the lip split and bled an orchid of blood, she didn't fight back, she didn't break into tears, she didn't run away as she imagined she might when she saw such things in the *telenovelas*.

In her own home her parents had never raised a hand to each other or to their children. Although she admitted she may have been brought up a little leniently as an only daughter—*la consentida*, the princess—there were some things she would never tolerate. Ever.

Instead, when it happened the first time, when they were barely man and wife, she had been so stunned, it left her speechless, motionless, numb. She had done nothing but reach up to the heat on her mouth and stare at the blood on her hand as if even then she didn't understand.

She could think of nothing to say, said nothing. Just stroked the dark curls of the man who wept and would weep like a child, his tears of repentance and shame, this time and each.

The men at the ice house. From what she can tell, from the times during her first year when still a newlywed she is invited and accompanies her husband, sits mute beside their conversation, waits and sips a beer until it grows warm, twists a paper napkin into a knot, then another into a fan, one into a rose, nods her head, smiles, yawns, politely grins, laughs at the appropriate moments, leans against her husband's sleeve, tugs at his elbow, and finally becomes good at predicting where the talk will lead, from this Cleófilas concludes each is nightly trying to find the truth lying at the bottom of the bottle like a gold doubloon on the sea floor.

They want to tell each other what they want to tell themselves. But what is bumping like a helium balloon at the ceiling of the brain never finds its way out. It bubbles and rises, it gurgles in the throat, it rolls across the surface of the tongue, and erupts from the lips—a belch.

If they are lucky, there are tears at the end of the long night. At any given moment, the fists try to speak. They are dogs chasing their own tails before lying down to sleep, trying to find a way, a route, an out, and—finally—get some peace.

In the morning sometimes before he opens his eyes. Or after they have finished loving. Or at times when he is simply across from her at the table putting pieces of food into his mouth and chewing. Cleófilas thinks, This is the man I have waited my whole life for.

Not that he isn't a good man. She has to remind herself why she loves him when she changes the baby's Pampers, or when she mops the bathroom floor, or tries to make the curtains for the doorways without doors, or whiten the linen. Or wonder a little when he kicks the refrigerator and says he hates this shitty house and is going out where he won't be bothered with the baby's howling and her suspicious questions, and her requests to fix this and this and this because if she had any brains in her head she'd realize he's been up before the rooster earning his living to pay for the food in her belly and the roof over her head and would have to wake up again early the next day so why can't you just leave me in peace, woman.

He is not very tall, no, and he doesn't look like the men on the *telenovelas*. His face still scarred from acne. And he has a bit of a belly from all the beer he drinks. Well, he's always been husky.

This man who farts and belches and snores as well as laughs and kisses and holds her. Somehow this husband whose whiskers she finds each morning in the sink, whose shoes she must air each evening on the porch, this husband who cuts his fingernails in public, laughs loudly, curses like a man, and demands each course of dinner be served on a separate plate like at his mother's, as soon as he gets home, on time or late, and who doesn't care at all for music or *telenovelas* or romance or roses or the moon floating pearly over the *arroyo*, or through the bedroom window for that matter, shut the blinds and go back to sleep, this man, this father, this rival, this keeper, this lord, this master, this husband till kingdom come.

A doubt. Slender as a hair. A washed cup set back on the shelf wrong-side-up. Her lipstick, and body talc, and hairbrush all arranged in the bathroom a different way.

No. Her imagination. The house the same as always. Nothing.

Coming home from the hospital with her new son, her husband. Something comforting in discovering her house slippers beneath the bed, the faded housecoat where she left it on the bathroom hook. Her pillow. Their bed.

Sweet sweet homecoming. Sweet as the scent of face powder in the air, jasmine, sticky liquor.

Smudged fingerprint on the door. Crushed cigarette in a glass. Wrinkle in the brain crumpling to a crease.

Sometimes she thinks of her father's house. But how could she go back there? What a disgrace. What would the neighbors say? Coming home like that with one baby on her hip and one in the oven. Where's your husband?

The town of gossips. The town of dust and despair. Which she has traded for this town of gossips. This town of dust, despair. Houses farther apart perhaps, though no more privacy because of it. No leafy *zócalo* in the center of the town, though the murmur of talk is clear enough all the same. No huddled whispering on the church steps each Sunday. Because here the whispering begins at sunset at the ice house instead.

This town with its silly pride for a bronze pecan the size of a baby carriage in front of the city hall. TV repair shop, drugstore, hardware, dry cleaner's, chiropractor's, liquor store, bail bonds, empty storefront, and nothing, nothing, nothing of interest. Nothing one could walk to, at any rate. Because the towns here are built so that you have to depend on husbands. Or you stay home. Or you drive. If you're rich enough to own, allowed to drive, your own car.

There is no place to go. Unless one counts the neighbor ladies. Soledad on one side, Dolores on the other. Or the creek.

Don't go out there after dark, *mi'jita*. Stay near the house. *No es bueno para la salud. Mala suerte*. Bad luck. *Mal aire*. You'll get sick and the baby too. You'll catch a fright wandering about in the dark, and then you'll see how right we were.

The stream sometimes only a muddy puddle in the summer, though now in the springtime, because of the rains, a good-size alive thing, a thing with a voice all its own, all day and all night calling in its high, silver voice. Is it La Llorona, the weeping woman? La Llorona, who drowned her own children. Perhaps La Llorona is the one they named the creek after, she thinks, remembering all the stories she learned as a child.

La Llorona calling to her. She is sure of it. Cleófilas sets the baby's Donald Duck blanket on the grass. Listens. The day sky turning to night. The baby pulling up fistfuls of grass and laughing. La Llorona. Wonders if something as quiet as this drives a woman to the darkness under the trees.

What she needs is... and made a gesture as if to yank a woman's buttocks to his groin. Maximiliano, the foul-smelling fool from across the road, said this and set the men laughing, but Cleófilas just muttered. *Grosero,* and went on washing dishes.

She knew he said it not because it was true, but more because it was he who needed to sleep with a woman, instead of drinking each night at the ice house and stumbling home alone.

Maximiliano who was said to have killed his wife in an ice-house brawl when she came at him with a mop. I had to shoot, he had said—she was armed.

Their laughter outside the kitchen window. Her husband's, his friends'. Manolo, Beto, Efraín, el Perico. Maximiliano.

Was Cleófilas just exaggerating as her husband always said? It seemed the newspapers were full of such stories. This woman found on the side of the interstate. This one pushed from a moving car. This one's cadaver, this one unconscious, this one beaten blue. Her ex-husband, her husband, her lover, her father, her brother, her uncle, her friend, her co-worker. Always. The same grisly news in the pages of the dailies. She dunked a glass under the soapy water for a moment—shivered.

He had thrown a book. Hers. From across the room. A hot welt across the cheek. She could forgive that. But what stung more was the fact it was *her* book, a love story by Corín Tellado, what she loved most now that she lived in the U.S., without a television set, without the *telenovelas*.

Except now and again when her husband was away and she could manage it, the few episodes glimpsed at the neighbor lady Soledad's house because Dolores didn't care for that sort of thing, though Soledad was often kind enough to retell what had happened on what episode of *María de Nadie,* the poor Argentine country girl who had the ill fortune of falling in love with the beautiful son of the Arrocha family, the very family she worked for, whose roof she slept under and whose floors she vacuumed, while in that same house, with the dust brooms and floor cleaners as witnesses, the square-jawed Juan Carlos Arrocha had uttered words of love, I love you, María, listen to me, *mi querida,* but it was she who had to say No, no, we are not of the same class, and remind him it was not his place nor hers to fall in love, while all the while her heart was breaking, can you imagine.

Cleófilas thought her life would have to be like that, like a *telenovela,* only now the episodes got sadder and sadder. And there were no commercials in between for comic relief. And no happy ending in sight. She thought this when she sat with the baby out by the creek behind the house. Cleófilas de . . . ? But somehow she would have to change her name to Topazio, or Yesenia, Cristal, Adriana, Stefania, Andrea, something more poetic than Cleófilas. Everything happened to women with names like jewels. But what happened to a Cleófilas? Nothing. But a crack in the face.

Because the doctor has said so. She has to go. To make sure the new baby is all right, so there won't be any problems when he's born, and the appointment card says next Tuesday. Could he please take her. And that's all.

No, she won't mention it. She promises. If the doctor asks she can say she fell down the front steps or slipped when she was out in the backyard, slipped out back, she could tell him that. She has to go back next Tuesday, Juan Pedro, please, for the new baby. For their child.

She could write to her father and ask maybe for money, just a loan, for the new baby's medical expenses. Well then if he'd rather she didn't. All right, she won't. Please don't anymore. Please don't. She knows it's difficult saving money with all the bills they have, but how else are they going to get out of debt with the truck payments? And after the rent and the food and the electricity and the gas and the water and the who-knows-what, well, there's hardly anything left. But please, at least for the doctor visit. She won't ask for anything else. She has to. Why is she so anxious? Because.

Because she is going to make sure the baby is not turned around backward this time to split her down the center. Yes. Next Tuesday at five-thirty. I'll have Juan Pedrito dressed and ready. But those are the only shoes he has. I'll polish them, and we'll be ready. As soon as you come from work. We won't make you ashamed.

Felice? It's me, Graciela.

No, I can't talk louder. I'm at work.

Look, I need kind of a favor. There's a patient, a lady here who's got a problem.

Well, wait a minute. Are you listening to me or what?

I can't talk real loud 'cause her husband's in the next room.

Well, would you just listen?

I was going to do this sonogram on her—she's pregnant, right?—and she just starts crying on me. *Híjole,* Felice! This poor lady's got black-and-blue marks all over. I'm not kidding.

From her husband. Who else? Another one of those brides from across the border. And her family's all in Mexico.

Shit. You think they're going to help her? Give me a break. This lady doesn't even speak English. She hasn't been allowed to call home or write or nothing. That's why I'm calling you.

She needs a ride.

Not to Mexico, you goof. Just to the Greyhound. In San Anto.

No, just a ride. She's got her own money. All you'd have to do is drop her off in San Antonio on your way home. Come on, Felice. Please? If we don't help her, who will? I'd drive her myself, but she needs to be on that bus before her husband gets home from work. What do you say?

I don't know. Wait.

Right away, tomorrow even.

Well, if tomorrow's no good for you . . .

It's a date, Felice. Thursday. At the Cash N Carry off I-10. Noon. She'll be ready.

Oh, and her name's Cleófilas.

I don't know. One of those Mexican saints, I guess. A martyr or something.

Cleófilas. C-L-E-O-F-I-L-A-S. Cle. O. Fi. Las. Write it down.

Thanks, Felice. When her kid's born she'll have to name her after us, right?

Yeah, you got it. A regular soap opera sometimes. *Qué vida, comadre. Bueno* bye.

All morning that flutter of half-fear, half-doubt. At any moment Juan Pedro might appear in the doorway. On the street. At the Cash N Carry. Like in the dreams she dreamed.

There was that to think about, yes, until the woman in the pickup drove up. Then there wasn't time to think about anything but the pickup pointed toward San Antonio. Put your bags in the back and get in.

But when they drove across the *arroyo,* the driver opened her mouth and let out a yell as loud as any mariachi. Which startled not only Cleófilas, but Juan Pedrito as well.

Pues, look how cute. I scared you two, right? Sorry. Should've warned you. Every time I cross that bridge I do that. Because of the name, you know. Woman Hollering. *Pues,* I holler. She said this in a Spanish pocked with English and laughed. Did you ever notice, Felice continued, how nothing around here is named after a woman? Really. Unless she's the Virgin. I guess you're only famous if you're a virgin. She was laughing again.

That's why I like the name of that *arroyo.* Makes you want to holler like Tarzan, right?

Everything about this woman, this Felice, amazed Cleófilas. The fact that she drove a pickup. A pickup, mind you, but when Cleófilas asked if it was her husband's, she said she didn't have a husband. The pickup was hers. She herself had chosen it. She herself was paying for it.

I used to have a Pontiac Sunbird. But those cars are for *viejas.* Pussy cars. Now this here is a *real* car.

What kind of talk was that coming from a woman? Cleófilas

thought. But then again, Felice was like no woman she'd ever met. Can you imagine, when we crossed the *arroyo* she just started yelling like a crazy, she would say later to her father and brothers. Just like that. Who would've thought?

Who would've? Pain or rage, perhaps, but not a hoot like the one Felice had just let go. Makes you want to holler like Tarzan, Felice had said.

Then Felice began laughing again, but it wasn't Felice laughing. It was gurgling out of her own throat, a long ribbon of laughter, like water.

The Marlboro Man

Durango was his name. Not his *real* name. I don't remember his real name, but it'll come to me. I've got it in my phone book at home. My girlfriend Romelia used to live with him. You *know* her, in fact. The real pretty one with big lips who came over to our table at the Beauregards' once when the Number Two Dinners were playing.

The one with the ponytail?

No. Her friend. Anyway, she lived with him for a year even though he was *way* too old for her.

For real? But I thought the Marlboro Man was gay.

He *was*? Romelia never told me *that*.

Yeah. In fact, I'm positive. I remember because I had a bad-ass crush on him, and one day I see a commercial for *60 Minutes*, right?

SPECIAL. TONIGHT! THE MARLBORO MAN. I remember saying to myself, Hot damn, I can't miss that.

Maybe Romelia *did* insinuate, but I didn't pick up on it.

What's his name? That guy from *60 Minutes*.

Andy Rooney?

Not Andy Rooney, *girl*friend! The other guy. The one that looks sad all the time.

Dan Rather.

Yeah, him. Dan Rather interviewed him on *60 Minutes*. You know, "Whatever happened to the Marlboro Man" and all that shit. Dan Rather interviewed him. The Marlboro Man was working as an AIDS clinic volunteer and he died from it even.

No, he didn't. He died from cancer. Too many cigarettes, I guess.

Are we talking about the same Marlboro Man?

He and Romelia lived on this fabulous piece of real estate in the hill country, outside Fredericksburg. Beautiful house on a bluff, next to some cattle ranches. You'd think you were miles from civilization, deer and wild turkey and roadrunners and hawks and all that, but it was only a ten-minute drive to town. They had a big Fourth of July party there once and invited everybody who was anybody. Willie Nelson, Esteban Jordán, Augie Meyers, all that crowd.

No kidding.

He had this habit of taking off all his clothes in public. I ran into them once at the Liberty, and he was dressed up in this luscious suit. Very *GQ,* know what I mean? *Très élégant.* Well, I waved to Romelia, meaning to go over to the bar later and say hi. But by the time I got to my pecan pie, he was already marching out the door wearing nothing but a cocktail napkin. I swear, he was *some*thing.

GOD! Don't kill me. I used to dream he'd be the father of my children.

Well, yeah. That is if we're talking about the same Marlboro Man. There've been lots of Marlboro Men. Just like there've been lots of Lassies, and lots of Shamu the Whale, and lots of Ralph the Swimming Pig. Well, what did you think, girlfriend? *All* those billboards. *All* those years!

Did he have a mustache?

Yeah.

And did he play bit parts in Clint Eastwood westerns?

I think so. At least he played in some Wells Fargo things that I know of.

And was he originally from northern California, used to have a little brother who was borderline mentally retarded, did some porno flicks before Marlboro discovered him?

Well, all I know is he was called Durango. And he owned a ranch out in the hill country that once belonged to Lady Bird Johnson. And he and some friends of the Texas Tornadoes lost a lot of money investing in some recording studio that was supposed to have thirty-six tracks instead of the usual sixteen, or whatever. And he gave Romelia hell, always chasing any young *thang* that wore a skirt and . . .

But Dan Rather said he was the *original* Marlboro Man.

The original, huh? . . . Well, maybe the one I'm talking about who lived with Romelia wasn't the *real* Marlboro Man. . . . But he *was* old.

La Fabulosa: A Texas Operetta

She likes to say she's "Spanish," but she's from Laredo like the rest of us—or "Lardo," as we call it. Her name is Berriozábal. Carmen. Worked as a secretary for a San Antonio law firm.

Big *chichis*. I mean big. Men couldn't take their eyes off them. She couldn't help it, really. Anytime they talked to her they never looked her in the eye. It was kind of sad.

She kept this corporal at Fort Sam Houston. Young. A looker. José Arrambide. He had a high school honey back home who sold nachos at the mall, still waiting for him to come back to Harlingen, marry her, and buy that three-piece bedroom set on layaway. Dream on, right?

Well, this José wasn't Carmen's LUH-uv of her life. Just her San Antonio "thang," so to speak. But you know how men are. Unless you're washing their feet and drying them with your hair, they just can't take it. I mean it. And Carmen was a take-it-or-leave-it type of woman. If you don't like it, there's the door. Like that. She was something.

Not smart. I mean, she didn't know enough to get her teeth

cleaned every year, or to buy herself a duplex. But the corporal was hooked. Her genuine guaranteed love slave. I don't know why, but when you treat men bad, they love it.

Yeah, sure, he was her sometime sweetheart, but what's that to a woman who's twenty and got the world by the eggs. First chance, she took up with a famous Texas senator who was paving his way to the big house. Set her up in a fancy condo in north Austin. Camilo Escamilla. You maybe might've heard of him.

When José found out, it was a big *escándalo,* as they say. Tried to kill her. Tried to kill himself. But this Camilo kept it out of the papers. He was that important. And besides, he had a wife and kids who posed with him every year for the calendar he gave away at Christmas. He wasn't about to throw his career out the window for no *fulanita*.

According to who you talk to, you hear different. José's friends say he left his initials across those famous *chichis* with a knife, but that sure sounds like talk, don't it?

I heard he went AWOL. Became a bullfighter in Matamoros, just so he could die like a man. Somebody else said *she's* the one who wants to die.

Don't you believe it. She ran off with King Kong Cárdenas, a professional wrestler from Crystal City and a sweetie. I know her cousin Lerma, and we saw her just last week at the Floore Country Store in Helotes. Hell, she bought us a beer, two-stepped and twirled away to "Hey Baby Qué Pasó."

Remember the Alamo

Gustavo Galindo, Ernie Sepúlveda, Jessie Robles, Jr., Ronnie DeHoyos, Christine Zamora . . .

When I was a kid and my ma added the rice to the hot oil, you know how it sizzles and spits, it sounds kind of like applause, right? Well, I'd always bow and say *Gracias, mi querido público*, thank you, and blow kisses to an imaginary crowd. I still do, kind of as a joke. When I make Spanish rice or something and add it to the oil. It roars, and I bow, just a little so no one would guess, but I bow, and I'm still blowing kisses, only inside.

Mary Alice Luján, Santiago Sanabria, Timoteo Herrera . . .

But I'm not Rudy when I perform. I mean, I'm not Rudy Cantú from Falfurrias anymore. I'm Tristán. Every Thursday night at the Travisty. Behind the Alamo, you can't miss it. One-man show, girl. Flamenco, salsa, tango, fandango, merengue, cumbia, cha-cha-chá. Don't forget. The Travisty. Remember the Alamo.

Lionel Ontiveros, Darlene Limón, Alex Vigil . . .

There are other performers, the mambo queens—don't get me wrong, it's not that they're not good at what they do. But they're not class acts. Daniela Romo impersonators. Lucha Villa look-alikes. Carmen Mirandas. Fruit department, if you ask me. But Tristán is very—how do I put it?—elegant. I mean, when he walks down the street, he turns heads like this. Passionate and stormy. And arrogant. Yes, arrogant a little. Sweetheart, in this business you have to be.

Blás G. Cortinas, Armando Salazar, Freddie Mendoza . . .

Tristán holds himself like a matador. His clothes magnificent. Absolutely perfect, like a second skin. The crowd throbbing—Tris-TAN, Tris-TAN, Tris-TAN!!! Tristán smiles, the room shivers. He raises his arms, the wings of a hawk. Spotlight clean as the moon of Andalucía. Audience breathless as water. And then . . . *Boom!* The heels like shotguns. A dance till death. I will love you *hasta la muerte, mi vida.* Do you hear? Until death.

Brenda Núñez, Jacinto Tovar, Henry Bautista, Nancy Rose Luna . . .

Because every Thursday night Tristán dances with La Calaca Flaca. Tristán takes the fag hag by the throat and throttles her senseless. Tristán's not afraid of La Flaquita, Thin Death.

Arturo Domínguez, Porfiria Escalante, Gregory Gallegos Durán, Ralph G. Soliz . . .

Tristán leads Death across the floor. *¿Verdad que me quieres, mi cariñito, verdad que sí? Hasta la muerte.* I'll show you how to ache.

Paul Villareal Saucedo, Monica Riojas, Baltazar M. López . . .

Say it. Say you want me. You want me. *Te quiero.* Look at me. I said *look* at me. *Don't* take your eyes from mine, Death. Yesssss. My treasure. My precious. *Mi pedacito de alma desnuda.* You want me so bad it hurts. A tug-of-war, a tease and stroke. Smoke in the mouth. *Hasta la muerte.* Ha!

Dorotea Villalobos, Jorge H. Hull, Aurora Anguiano Román, Amado Tijerina, Bobby Mendiola . . .

Tristán's family? They love him no matter what. His ma proud of his fame—That's my *m'ijo.* His sisters jealous because he's the pretty one. But they adore him, and he gives them tips on their makeup.

At first his father said What's this? But then when the newspaper articles started pouring in, well, what could he do but send photocopies to the relatives in Mexico, right? And Tristán sends them all free backstage passes. They drive all the way from the Valley for the opening of the show. Even the snooty relatives from Monterrey. It's unbelievable. Last time he invited his family they took the whole damn third floor of La Mansión del Rio. I'm not kidding.

He's the greatest live act in San Anto. Doesn't put up with bull. No way. Either loves you or hates you. Ferocious, I'm telling you. *Muy* hot-hot-hot or cold as a witch's tough *chichi.* Isn't tight with nobody but family and friends. Doesn't need to be. Go on, say it. I want you to. I'll school you. I'll show you how it's done.

See this ring? A gift from an art admirer and dance aficionado. Sent $500 worth of red roses the night of his opening. You should've seen the dressing room. Roses, roses, roses. Honey! Then he sent the ring, little diamonds set in the shape of Texas. Just because he was fond of art. That's how it is. Say it. *Te quiero*. Say you want me. You want me.

The bitch and Tristán are like this. La Flaca crazy about him. Lots of people love Tristán like that. Because Tristán dares to be different. To stand out in a crowd. To have style and grace. And *elegancia*. Tristán has that kind of appeal.

He's not scared of the low-rider types who come up at the Esquire Bar, that beer-stinking, piss-soaked hole, jukebox screaming Brenda Lee's "I'm Sorry." *¿Eres maricón?* You a fag? Gives them a look like the edge of a razor across lip.

Dresses all in white in the summer, all in black in the winter. No in-between except for the show. That's how he is. Tristán. But he's never going to be anything but honest. Carry his heart in his hand. You know it.

And when he loves, gives himself body and soul. None of this fooling around. A love so complete you have to be ready for it. Courageous. Put on your seat belt, sweets. A ride to the finish. So bad it aches.

A dance until death. Every Thursday night when he glides with La Flaca. Wraps his arms around her. La Muertita with her shit-eating, bless-her-heart grin. Doesn't faze him. La Death with her dress up the crack of her ass. The girl's pathetic.

What a pair! The two like Ginger and Fred tangoing across the floor. Two angels, heavenly bodies floating cheek to cheek. Or *nalga* to *nalga*. Ay, girl, I'm telling you. *Wáchale, muchacha*. With those maracas and the cha-cha-chá of those bones-bones-bones, she's a natural. *¿Verdad que me quieres, mi cariñito? ¿Verdad que sí?*

Tristán? Never feels better than on Thursday nights when he's working her. When he's living those moments, the audience breathing, sighing out there, roaring when the curtains go up and the lights and music begin. That's when Tristán's life starts. Without ulcers or gas stations or hospital bills or bloody sheets or pubic hairs in the sink. Lovers in your arms pulling farther and farther away from you. Dried husks, hulls, coffee cups. Letters home sent back unopened.

Tristán's got nothing to do with the ugly, the ordinary. With screen doors with broken screens or peeling paint or raw hallways. The dirty backyards, the muddy spittle in the toilet you don't want to remember. Sweating, pressing himself against you, pink pink peepee blind and seamless as an eye, pink as a baby rat, your hand small and rubbing it, yes, like this, like so, and your skull being crushed by that sour smell and the taste like tears inside your sore mouth.

No. Tristán doesn't have memories like that. Only *amor del corazón*, that you can't buy, right? That is never used to hurt anybody. Never ashamed. Love like a body that wants to give and give of itself, that wants to create a universe where nothing is dirty, no one is hurting, no one sick, that's what Tristán thinks of when he dances.

Mario Pacheco, Ricky Estrada, Lillian Alvarado . . .

Say it. Say you want me. *Te quiero.* Like I want you. Say you love me. Like I love you. I love you. *Te quiero, mi querido público. Te adoro.* With all my heart. With my heart and with my body.

Ray Agustín Huerta, Elsa González, Frank Castro, Abelardo Romo, Rochell M. Garza, Nacianceno Cavazos, Nelda Therese Flores, Roland Guillermo Pedraza, Renato Villa, Filemón Guzmán, Suzie A. Ybañez, David Mondragón . . .

This body.

Never Marry a Mexican

Never marry a Mexican, my ma said once and always. She said this because of my father. She said this though she was Mexican too. But she was born here in the U.S., and he was born there, and it's *not* the same, you know.

I'll *never* marry. Not any man. I've known men too intimately. I've witnessed their infidelities, and I've helped them to it. Unzipped and unhooked and agreed to clandestine maneuvers. I've been accomplice, committed premeditated crimes. I'm guilty of having caused deliberate pain to other women. I'm vindictive and cruel, and I'm capable of anything.

I admit, there was a time when all I wanted was to belong to a man. To wear that gold band on my left hand and be worn on his arm like an expensive jewel brilliant in the light of day. Not the sneaking around I did in different bars that all looked the same, red carpets with a black grillwork design, flocked wallpaper, wooden wagon-wheel light fixtures with hurricane lampshades a sick amber color like the drinking glasses you get for free at gas stations.

Dark bars, dark restaurants then. And if not—my apartment,

with his toothbrush firmly planted in the toothbrush holder like a flag on the North Pole. The bed so big because he never stayed the whole night. Of course not.

Borrowed. That's how I've had my men. Just the cream skimmed off the top. Just the sweetest part of the fruit, without the bitter skin that daily living with a spouse can rend. They've come to me when they wanted the sweet meat then.

So, no. I've never married and never will. Not because I couldn't, but because I'm too romantic for marriage. Marriage has failed me, you could say. Not a man exists who hasn't disappointed me, whom I could trust to love the way I've loved. It's because I believe too much in marriage that I don't. Better to not marry than live a lie.

Mexican men, forget it. For a long time the men clearing off the tables or chopping meat behind the butcher counter or driving the bus I rode to school every day, those weren't men. Not men I considered as potential lovers. Mexican, Puerto Rican, Cuban, Chilean, Colombian, Panamanian, Salvadorean, Bolivian, Honduran, Argentine, Dominican, Venezuelan, Guatemalan, Ecuadorean, Nicaraguan, Peruvian, Costa Rican, Paraguayan, Uruguayan, I don't care. I never saw them. My mother did this to me.

I guess she did it to spare me and Ximena the pain she went through. Having married a Mexican man at seventeen. Having had to put up with all the grief a Mexican family can put on a girl because she was from *el otro lado,* the other side, and my father had married down by marrying her. If he had married a white woman from *el otro lado,* that would've been different. That would've been marrying up, even if the white girl was poor. But what could be more ridiculous than a Mexican girl who couldn't even speak Spanish, who didn't know enough to set a separate plate for each course at dinner, nor how to fold cloth napkins, nor how to set the silverware.

In my ma's house the plates were always stacked in the center of the table, the knives and forks and spoons standing in a jar, help yourself. All the dishes chipped or cracked and nothing matched. And no tablecloth, ever. And newspapers set on the table whenever my grandpa sliced watermelons, and how embarrassed she would be when her boyfriend, my father, would come over and there were newspapers all over the kitchen floor and table. And my grandpa, big hardworking Mexican man, saying Come, come and eat, and slicing a big wedge of those dark green watermelons, a big slice, he wasn't stingy with food. Never, even during the Depression. Come, come and eat, to whoever came knocking on the back door. Hobos sitting at the dinner table and the children staring and staring. Because my grandfather always made sure they never went without. Flour and rice, by the barrel and by the sack. Potatoes. Big bags of pinto beans. And watermelons, bought three or four at a time, rolled under his bed and brought out when you least expected. My grandpa had survived three wars, one Mexican, two American, and he knew what living without meant. He knew.

My father, on the other hand, did not. True, when he first came to this country he had worked shelling clams, washing dishes, planting hedges, sat on the back of the bus in Little Rock and had the bus driver shout, You—sit up here, and my father had shrugged sheepishly and said, No speak English.

But he was no economic refugee, no immigrant fleeing a war. My father ran away from home because he was afraid of facing his father after his first-year grades at the university proved he'd spent more time fooling around than studying. He left behind a house in Mexico City that was neither poor nor rich, but thought itself better than both. A boy who would get off a bus when he saw a girl he knew board if he didn't have the money to pay her fare. That was the world my father left behind.

I imagine my father in his *fanfarrón* clothes, because that's what he was, a *fanfarrón*. That's what my mother thought the moment she turned around to the voice that was asking her to dance. A big show-off, she'd say years later. Nothing but a big show-off. But she never said why she married him. My father in his shark-blue suits with the starched handkerchief in the breast pocket, his felt fedora, his tweed topcoat with the big shoulders, and heavy British wing tips with the pin-hole design on the heel and toe. Clothes that cost a lot. Expensive. That's what my father's things said. *Calidad.* Quality.

My father must've found the U.S. Mexicans very strange, so foreign from what he knew at home in Mexico City where the servant served watermelon on a plate with silverware and a cloth napkin, or mangos with their own special prongs. Not like this, eating with your legs wide open in the yard, or in the kitchen hunkered over newspapers. *Come, come and eat.* No, never like this.

How I make my living depends. Sometimes I work as a translator. Sometimes I get paid by the word and sometimes by the hour, depending on the job. I do this in the day, and at night I paint. I'd do anything in the day just so I can keep on painting.

I work as a substitute teacher, too, for the San Antonio Independent School District. And that's worse than translating those travel brochures with their tiny print, believe me. I can't stand kids. Not any age. But it pays the rent.

Any way you look at it, what I do to make a living is a form of prostitution. People say, "A painter? How nice," and want to invite me to their parties, have me decorate the lawn like an exotic orchid for hire. But do they buy art?

I'm amphibious. I'm a person who doesn't belong to any class. The rich like to have me around because they envy my creativity; they know they can't buy *that.* The poor don't mind if I live in their neighborhood because they know I'm poor like they are, even if my education and the way I dress keeps us worlds apart. I don't belong to any class. Not to the poor, whose neighborhood I share. Not to the rich, who come to my exhibitions and buy my work. Not to the middle class from which my sister Ximena and I fled.

When I was young, when I first left home and rented that apartment with my sister and her kids right after her husband left, I thought it would be glamorous to be an artist. I wanted to be like Frida or Tina. I was ready to suffer with my camera and my paint brushes in that awful apartment we rented for $150 each because it had high ceilings and those wonderful glass skylights that convinced us we had to have it. Never mind there was no sink in the bathroom, and a tub that looked like a sarcophagus, and floorboards that didn't meet, and a hallway to scare away the dead. But fourteen-foot ceilings was enough for us to write a check for the deposit right then and there. We thought it all romantic. You know the place, the one on Zarzamora on top of the barber shop with the Casasola prints of the Mexican Revolution. Neon BIRRIA TEPATITLÁN sign round the corner, two goats knocking their heads together, and all those Mexican bakeries, Las Brisas for *huevos rancheros* and *carnitas* and *barbacoa* on Sundays, and fresh fruit milk shakes, and mango *paletas,* and more signs in Spanish than in English. We thought it was great, great. The barrio looked cute in the daytime, like Sesame Street. Kids hopscotching on the sidewalk, blessed little boogers. And hardware stores that still sold ostrich-feather dusters, and whole families marching out of Our Lady of Guadalupe Church on Sundays, girls in their swirly-whirly dresses and patent-leather shoes, boys in their dress Stacys and shiny shirts.

But nights, that was nothing like what we knew up on the north side. Pistols going off like the wild, wild West, and me and Ximena and the kids huddled in one bed with the lights off listening to it all, saying, Go to sleep, babies, it's just firecrackers. But we knew better. Ximena would say, Clemencia, maybe we should go home.

And I'd say, Shit! Because she knew as well as I did there was no home to go home to. Not with our mother. Not with that man she married. After Daddy died, it was like we didn't matter. Like Ma was so busy feeling sorry for herself, I don't know. I'm not like Ximena. I still haven't worked it out after all this time, even though our mother's dead now. My half brothers living in that house that should've been ours, me and Ximena's. But that's—how do you say it?—water under the damn? I can't ever get the sayings right even though I was born in this country. We didn't say shit like that in our house.

Once Daddy was gone, it was like my ma didn't exist, like if she died, too. I used to have a little finch, twisted one of its tiny red legs between the bars of the cage once, who knows how. The leg just dried up and fell off. My bird lived a long time without it, just a little red stump of a leg. He was fine, really. My mother's memory is like that, like if something already dead dried up and fell off, and I stopped missing where she used to be. Like if I never had a mother. And I'm not ashamed to say it either. When she married that white man, and he and his boys moved into my father's house, it was as if she stopped being my mother. Like I never even had one.

Ma always sick and too busy worrying about her own life, she would've sold us to the Devil if she could. "Because I married so young, *mi'ja*," she'd say. "Because your father, he was so much older than me, and I never had a chance to be young. Honey, try to understand . . ." Then I'd stop listening.

That man she met at work, Owen Lambert, the foreman at the photo-finishing plant, who she was seeing even while my father was sick. Even then. That's what I can't forgive.

When my father was coughing up blood and phlegm in the hospital, half his face frozen, and his tongue so fat he couldn't talk, he looked so small with all those tubes and plastic sacks dangling around him. But what I remember most is the smell, like death was already sitting on his chest. And I remember the doctor scraping the phlegm out of my father's mouth with a white washcloth, and my daddy gagging and I wanted to yell, Stop, you stop that, he's my daddy. Goddamn you. Make him live. Daddy, don't. Not yet, not yet, not yet. And how I couldn't hold myself up, I couldn't hold myself up. Like if they'd beaten me, or pulled my insides out through my nostrils, like if they'd stuffed me with cinnamon and cloves, and I just stood there dry-eyed next to Ximena and my mother, Ximena between us because I wouldn't let her stand next to me. Everyone repeating over and over the Ave Marías and Padre Nuestros. The priest sprinkling holy water, *mundo sin fin, amén*.

Drew, remember when you used to call me your Malinalli? It was a joke, a private game between us, because you looked like a Cortez with that beard of yours. My skin dark against yours. Beautiful, you said. You said I was beautiful, and when you said it, Drew, I was.

My Malinalli, Malinche, my courtesan, you said, and yanked my head back by the braid. Calling me that name in between little gulps of breath and the raw kisses you gave, laughing from that black beard of yours.

Before daybreak, you'd be gone, same as always, before I even knew it. And it was as if I'd imagined you, only the teeth marks on my belly and nipples proving me wrong.

Your skin pale, but your hair blacker than a pirate's. Malinalli, you called me, remember? *Mi doradita*. I liked when you spoke to me in my language. I could love myself and think myself worth loving.

Your son. Does he know how much I had to do with his birth? I was the one who convinced you to let him be born. Did you tell him, while his mother lay on her back laboring his birth, I lay in his mother's bed making love to you.

You're nothing without me. I created you from spit and red dust. And I can snuff you between my finger and thumb if I want to. Blow you to kingdom come. You're just a smudge of paint I chose to birth on canvas. And when I made you over, you were no longer a part of her, you were all mine. The landscape of your body taut as a drum. The heart beneath that hide thrumming and thrumming. Not an inch did I give back.

I paint and repaint you the way I see fit, even now. After all these years. Did you know that? Little fool. You think I went hobbling along with my life, whimpering and whining like some twangy country-and-western when you went back to her. But I've been waiting. Making the world look at you from my eyes. And if that's not power, what is?

Nights I light all the candles in the house, the ones to La Virgen de Guadalupe, the ones to El Niño Fidencio, Don Pedrito Jaramillo, Santo Niño de Atocha, Nuestra Señora de San Juan de los Lagos, and especially, Santa Lucía, with her beautiful eyes on a plate.

Your eyes are beautiful, you said. You said they were the darkest eyes you'd ever seen and kissed each one as if they were capable of miracles. And after you left, I wanted to scoop them out with a spoon, place them on a plate under these blue blue skies, food for the blackbirds.

The boy, your son. The one with the face of that redheaded woman who is your wife. The boy red-freckled like fish food floating on the skin of water. That boy.

I've been waiting patient as a spider all these years, since I was nineteen and he was just an idea hovering in his mother's head, and I'm the one that gave him permission and made it happen, see.

Because your father wanted to leave your mother and live with me. Your mother whining for a child, at least *that*. And he kept saying, Later, we'll see, later. But all along it was me he wanted to be with, it was me, he said.

I want to tell you this evenings when you come to see me. When you're full of talk about what kind of clothes you're going to buy, and what you used to be like when you started high school and what you're like now that you're almost finished. And how everyone knows you as a rocker, and your band, and your new red guitar that you just got because your mother gave you a choice, a guitar or a car, but you don't need a car, do you, because I drive you everywhere. You could be my son if you weren't so light-skinned.

This happened. A long time ago. Before you were born. When you were a moth inside your mother's heart, I was your father's student, yes, just like you're mine now. And your father painted and painted me, because he said, I was his *doradita,* all golden and sun-baked, and that's the kind of woman he likes best, the ones brown as river sand, yes. And he took me under his wing and in his bed, this man, this teacher, your father. I was honored that he'd done me the favor. I was that young.

All I know is I was sleeping with your father the night you were born. In the same bed where you were conceived. I was sleeping with your father and didn't give a damn about that woman, your mother. If she was a brown woman like me, I might've had a harder time living with myself, but since she's not, I don't care. I was there first, always. I've always been there, in the mirror, under his skin, in the blood, before you were born. And he's been here in my heart before I even knew him. Understand? He's always been here. Always. Dissolving like a hibiscus flower, exploding like a rope into dust. I don't care what's right anymore. I don't care about his wife. She's not *my* sister.

And it's not the last time I've slept with a man the night his wife is birthing a baby. Why do I do that, I wonder? Sleep with a man when his wife is giving life, being suckled by a thing with its eyes still shut. Why do that? It's always given me a bit of crazy joy to be able to kill those women like that, without their knowing it. To know I've had their husbands when they were anchored in blue hospital rooms, their guts yanked inside out, the baby sucking their breasts while their husband sucked mine. All this while their ass stitches were still hurting.

Once, drunk on margaritas, I telephoned your father at four in the morning, woke the bitch up. Hello, she chirped. I want to talk to Drew. Just a moment, she said in her most polite drawing-room English. Just a moment. I laughed about that for weeks. What a stupid ass to pass the phone over to the lug asleep beside her. Excuse me, honey, it's for you. When Drew mumbled hello I was laughing so hard I could hardly talk. Drew? That dumb bitch of a wife of yours, I said, and that's all I could manage. That stupid stupid stupid. No Mexican woman would react like that. Excuse me, honey. It cracked me up.

He's got the same kind of skin, the boy. All the blue veins pale and clear just like his mama. Skin like roses in December. Pretty boy. Little clone. Little cells split into you and you and you. Tell me, baby, which part of you is your mother. I try to imagine her lips, her jaw, her long long legs that wrapped themselves around this father who took me to his bed.

This happened. I'm asleep. Or pretend to be. You're watching me, Drew. I feel your weight when you sit on the corner of the bed, dressed and ready to go, but now you're just watching me sleep. Nothing. Not a word. Not a kiss. Just sitting. You're taking me in, under inspection. What do you think already?

I haven't stopped dreaming you. Did you know that? Do you

think it's strange? I never tell, though. I keep it to myself like I do all the thoughts I think of you.

After all these years.

I don't want you looking at me. I don't want you taking me in while I'm asleep. I'll open my eyes and frighten you away.

There. What did I tell you? *Drew? What is it?* Nothing. I'd knew you'd say that.

Let's not talk. We're no good at it. With you I'm useless with words. As if somehow I had to learn to speak all over again, as if the words I needed haven't been invented yet. We're cowards. Come back to bed. At least there I feel I have you for a little. For a moment. For a catch of the breath. You let go. You ache and tug. You rip my skin.

You're almost not a man without your clothes. How do I explain it? You're so much a child in my bed. Nothing but a big boy who needs to be held. I won't let anyone hurt you. My pirate. My slender boy of a man.

After all these years.

I didn't imagine it, did I? A Ganges, an eye of the storm. For a little. When we forgot ourselves, you tugged me, I leapt inside you and split you like an apple. Opened for the other to look and not give back. Something wrenched itself loose. Your body doesn't lie. It's not silent like you.

You're nude as a pearl. You've lost your train of smoke. You're tender as rain. If I'd put you in my mouth you'd dissolve like snow.

You were ashamed to be so naked. Pulled back. But I saw you for what you are, when you opened yourself for me. When you were careless and let yourself through. I caught that catch of the breath. I'm not crazy.

When you slept, you tugged me toward you. You sought me in the dark. I didn't sleep. Every cell, every follicle, every nerve, alert.

Watching you sigh and roll and turn and hug me closer to you. I didn't sleep. I was taking *you* in that time.

Your mother? Only once. Years after your father and I stopped seeing each other. At an art exhibition. A show on the photographs of Eugène Atget. Those images, I could look at them for hours. I'd taken a group of students with me.

It was your father I saw first. And in that instant I felt as if everyone in the room, all the sepia-toned photographs, my students, the men in business suits, the high-heeled women, the security guards, everyone, could see me for what I was. I had to scurry out, lead my kids to another gallery, but some things destiny has cut out for you.

He caught up with us in the coat-check area, arm in arm with a redheaded Barbie doll in a fur coat. One of those scary Dallas types, hair yanked into a ponytail, big shiny face like the women behind the cosmetic counters at Neiman's. That's what I remember. She must've been with him all along, only I swear I never saw her until that second.

You could tell from a slight hesitancy, only slight because he's too suave to hesitate, that he was nervous. Then he's walking toward me, and I didn't know what to do, just stood there dazed like those animals crossing the road at night when the headlights stun them.

And I don't know why, but all of a sudden I looked at my shoes and felt ashamed at how old they looked. And he comes up to me, my love, your father, in that way of his with that grin that makes me want to beat him, makes me want to make love to him, and he says in the most sincere voice you ever heard, "Ah, Clemencia! *This* is Megan." No introduction could've been meaner. *This* is Megan. Just like that.

I grinned like an idiot and held out my paw—"Hello, Megan"—

and smiled too much the way you do when you can't stand someone. Then I got the hell out of there, chattering like a monkey all the ride back with my kids. When I got home I had to lie down with a cold washcloth on my forehead and the TV on. All I could hear throbbing under the washcloth in that deep part behind my eyes: *This* is Megan.

And that's how I fell asleep, with the TV on and every light in the house burning. When I woke up it was something like three in the morning. I shut the lights and TV and went to get some aspirin, and the cats, who'd been asleep with me on the couch, got up too and followed me into the bathroom as if they knew what's what. And then they followed me into bed, where they aren't allowed, but this time I just let them, fleas and all.

This happened, too. I swear I'm not making this up. It's all true. It was the last time I was going to be with your father. We had agreed. All for the best. Surely I could see that, couldn't I? My own good. A good sport. A young girl like me. Hadn't I understood . . . responsibilities. Besides, he could *never* marry *me*. You didn't think . . . ? *Never marry a Mexican. Never marry a Mexican* . . . No, of course not. I see. I see.

We had the house to ourselves for a few days, who knows how. You and your mother had gone somewhere. Was it Christmas? I don't remember.

I remember the leaded-glass lamp with the milk glass above the dining-room table. I made a mental inventory of everything. The Egyptian lotus design on the hinges of the doors. The narrow, dark hall where your father and I had made love once. The four-clawed tub where he had washed my hair and rinsed it with a tin bowl. This window. That counter. The bedroom with its light in the morning, incredibly soft, like the light from a polished dime.

The house was immaculate, as always, not a stray hair anywhere, not a flake of dandruff or a crumpled towel. Even the roses on the dining-room table held their breath. A kind of airless cleanliness that always made me want to sneeze.

Why was I so curious about this woman he lived with? Every time I went to the bathroom, I found myself opening the medicine cabinet, looking at all the things that were hers. Her Estée Lauder lipsticks. Corals and pinks, of course. Her nail polishes—mauve was as brave as she could wear. Her cotton balls and blond hairpins. A pair of bone-colored sheepskin slippers, as clean as the day she'd bought them. On the door hook—a white robe with a MADE IN ITALY label, and a silky nightshirt with pearl buttons. I touched the fabrics. *Calidad.* Quality.

I don't know how to explain what I did next. While your father was busy in the kitchen, I went over to where I'd left my backpack, and took out a bag of gummy bears I'd bought. And while he was banging pots, I went around the house and left a trail of them in places I was sure *she* would find them. One in her lucite makeup organizer. One stuffed inside each bottle of nail polish. I untwisted the expensive lipsticks to their full length and smushed a bear on the top before recapping them. I even put a gummy bear in her diaphragm case in the very center of that luminescent rubber moon.

Why bother? Drew could take the blame. Or he could say it was the cleaning woman's Mexican voodoo. I knew that, too. It didn't matter. I got a strange satisfaction wandering about the house leaving them in places only she would look.

And just as Drew was shouting, "Dinner!" I saw it on the desk. One of those wooden babushka dolls Drew had brought her from his trip to Russia. I know. He'd bought one just like it for me.

I just did what I did, uncapped the doll inside a doll inside a doll, until I got to the very center, the tiniest baby inside all the others, and this I replaced with a gummy bear. And then I put the dolls back, just like I'd found them, one inside the other, inside the other. Except for the baby, which I put inside my pocket. All through dinner I kept reaching in the pocket of my jean jacket. When I touched it, it made me feel good.

On the way home, on the bridge over the *arroyo* on Guadalupe Street, I stopped the car, switched on the emergency blinkers, got out, and dropped the wooden toy into that muddy creek where winos piss and rats swim. The Barbie doll's toy stewing there in that muck. It gave me a feeling like nothing before and since.

Then I drove home and slept like the dead.

These mornings, I fix coffee for me, milk for the boy. I think of that woman, and I can't see a trace of my lover in this boy, as if she conceived him by immaculate conception.

I sleep with this boy, their son. To make the boy love me the way I love his father. To make him want me, hunger, twist in his sleep, as if he'd swallowed glass. I put him in my mouth. Here, little piece of my *corazón*. Boy with hard thighs and just a bit of down and a small hard downy ass like his father's, and that back like a valentine. Come here, *mi cariñito*. Come to *mamita*. Here's a bit of toast.

I can tell from the way he looks at me, I have him in my power. Come, sparrow. I have the patience of eternity. Come to *mamita*. My stupid little bird. I don't move. I don't startle him. I let him nibble. All, all for you. Rub his belly. Stroke him. Before I snap my teeth.

What is it inside me that makes me so crazy at 2 A.M.? I can't blame it on alcohol in my blood when there isn't any. It's something worse. Something that poisons the blood and tips me when the night swells and I feel as if the whole sky were leaning against my brain.

And if I killed someone on a night like this? And if it was *me* I killed instead, I'd be guilty of getting in the line of crossfire, innocent bystander, isn't it a shame. I'd be walking with my head full of images and my back to the guilty. Suicide? I couldn't say. I didn't see it.

Except it's not me who I want to kill. When the gravity of the planets is just right, it all tilts and upsets the visible balance. And that's when it wants to out from my eyes. That's when I get on the telephone, dangerous as a terrorist. There's nothing to do but let it come.

So. What do you think? Are you convinced now I'm as crazy as a tulip or a taxi? As vagrant as a cloud?

Sometimes the sky is so big and I feel so little at night. That's the problem with being cloud. The sky is so terribly big. Why is it worse at night, when I have such an urge to communicate and no language with which to form the words? Only colors. Pictures. And you know what I have to say isn't always pleasant.

Oh, love, there. I've gone and done it. What good is it? Good or bad, I've done what I had to do and needed to. And you've answered the phone, and startled me away like a bird. And now you're probably swearing under your breath and going back to sleep, with that wife beside you, warm, radiating her own heat, alive under the flannel and down and smelling a bit like milk and hand cream, and that smell familiar and dear to you, oh.

Human beings pass me on the street, and I want to reach out and strum them as if they were guitars. Sometimes all humanity strikes me as lovely. I just want to reach out and stroke someone, and say There, there, it's all right, honey. There, there, there.

Bread

We were hungry. We went into a bakery on Grand Avenue and bought bread. Filled the backseat. The whole car smelled of bread. Big sourdough loaves shaped like a fat ass. Fat-ass bread, I said in Spanish, *Nalgona* bread. Fat-ass bread, he said in Italian, but I forget how he said it.

We ripped big chunks with our hands and ate. The car a pearl blue like my heart that afternoon. Smell of warm bread, bread in both fists, a tango on the tape player loud, loud, loud, because me and him, we're the only ones who can stand it like that, like if the bandoneón, violin, piano, guitar, bass, were inside us, like when he wasn't married, like before his kids, like if all the pain hadn't passed between us.

Driving down streets with buildings that remind him, he says, how charming this city is. And me remembering when I was little, a cousin's baby who died from swallowing rat poison in a building like these.

That's just how it is. And that's how we drove. With all his new city memories and all my old. Him kissing me between big bites of bread.

Eyes of Zapata

I put my nose to your eyelashes. The skin of the eyelids as soft as the skin of the penis, the collarbone with its fluted wings, the purple knot of the nipple, the dark, blue-black color of your sex, the thin legs and long thin feet. For a moment I don't want to think of your past nor your future. For now you are here, you are mine.

Would it be right to tell you what I do each night you sleep here? After your cognac and cigar, after I'm certain you're asleep, I examine at my leisure your black trousers with the silver buttons—fifty-six pairs on each side; I've counted them—your embroidered sombrero with its horsehair tassel, the lovely Dutch linen shirt, the fine braid stitching on the border of your *charro* jacket, the handsome black boots, your tooled gun belt and silver spurs. Are you my general? Or only that boy I met at the country fair in San Lázaro?

Hands too pretty for a man. Elegant hands, graceful hands, fingers smelling sweet as your Havanas. I had pretty hands once, remember? You used to say I had the prettiest hands of any woman in Cuautla. *Exquisitas* you called them, as if they were something to eat. It still makes me laugh remembering that.

Ay, but now look. Nicked and split and callused—how is it the hands get old first? The skin as coarse as the wattle of a hen. It's from the planting in the *tlacolol,* from the hard man's work I do clearing the field with the hoe and the machete, dirty work that leaves the clothes filthy, work no woman would do before the war.

But I'm not afraid of hard work or of being alone in the hills. I'm not afraid of dying or jail. I'm not afraid of the night like other women who run to the sacristy at the first call of *el gobierno.* I'm not other women.

Look at you. Snoring already? *Pobrecito.* Sleep, *papacito.* There, there. It's only me—Inés. *Duerme, mi trigueño, mi chulito, mi bebito. Ya, ya, ya.*

You say you can't sleep anywhere like you sleep here. So tired of always having to be *el gran general* Emiliano Zapata. The nervous fingers flinch, the long elegant bones shiver and twitch. Always waiting for the assassin's bullet.

Everyone is capable of becoming a traitor, and traitors must be broken, you say. A horse to be broken. A new saddle that needs breaking in. To break a spirit. Something to whip and lasso like you did in the *jaripeos* years ago.

Everything bothers you these days. Any noise, any light, even the sun. You say nothing for hours, and then when you do speak, it's an outburst, a fury. Everyone afraid of you, even your men. You hide yourself in the dark. You go days without sleep. You don't laugh anymore.

I don't need to ask; I've seen for myself. The war is not going well. I see it in your face. How it's changed over the years, Miliano. From so much watching, the face grows that way. These wrinkles new, this furrow, the jaw clenched tight. Eyes creased from learning to see in the night.

They say the widows of sailors have eyes like that, from squinting into the line where the sky and sea dissolve. It's the same with us from all this war. We're all widows. The men as well as the women, even the children. All *clinging to the tail of the horse of our* jefe *Zapata.* All of us scarred from these nine years of *aguantando*—enduring.

Yes, it's in your face. It's always been there. Since before the war. Since before I knew you. Since your birth in Anenecuilco and even before then. Something hard and tender all at once in those eyes. You knew before any of us, didn't you?

This morning the messenger arrived with the news you'd be arriving before nightfall, but I was already boiling the corn for your supper tortillas. I saw you riding in on the road from Villa de Ayala. Just as I saw you that day in Anenecuilco when the revolution had just begun and the government was everywhere looking for you. You were worried about the land titles, went back to dig them up from where you'd hidden them eighteen months earlier, under the altar in the village church—am I right?—reminding Chico Franco to keep them safe. *I'm bound to die,* you said, *someday. But our titles stand to be guaranteed.*

I wish I could rub the grief from you as if it were a smudge on the cheek. I want to gather you up in my arms as if you were Nicolás or Malena, run up to the hills. I know every cave and crevice, every back road and ravine, but I don't know where I could hide you from yourself. You're tired. You're sick and lonely with this war, and I don't want any of those things to ever touch you again, Miliano. It's enough for now you are here. For now. Under my roof again.

Sleep, *papacito.* It's only Inés circling above you, wide-eyed all night. The sound of my wings like the sound of a velvet cape crumpling. A warm breeze against your skin, the wide expanse of moon-white feathers as if I could touch all the walls of the house at one sweep. A rustling, then weightlessness, light scattered out the window until it's the moist night wind beneath my owl wings. Whorl of stars like the filigree earrings you gave me. Your tired horse still as tin, there, where you tied it to a guamuchil tree. River singing louder than ever since the time of the rains.

I scout the hillsides, the mountains. My blue shadow over the high grass and slash of *barrancas,* over the ghosts of haciendas silent under the blue night. From this height, the village looks the same as before the war. As if the roofs were still intact, the walls still whitewashed, the cobbled streets swept of rubble and weeds. Nothing blistered and burnt. Our lives smooth and whole.

Round and round the blue countryside, over the scorched fields, giddy wind barely ruffling my stiff, white feathers, above the two soldiers you left guarding our door, one asleep, the other dull from a day of hard riding. But I'm awake, I'm always awake when you are here. Nothing escapes me. No coyote in the mountains, or scorpion in the sand. Everything clear. The trail you rode here. The night jasmine with its frothy scent of sweet milk. The makeshift roof of cane leaves on our adobe house. Our youngest child of five summers asleep in her hammock—*What a little woman you are now, Malenita.* The laughing sound of the river and canals, and the high, melancholy voice of the wind in the branches of the tall pine.

I slow-circle and glide into the house, bringing the night-wind smell with me, fold myself back into my body. I haven't left you. I don't leave you, not ever. Do you know why? Because when you are gone I re-create you from memory. The scent of your skin, the mole above the broom of your mustache, how you fit in my palms. Your skin dark and rich as *piloncillo.* This face in my hands. I miss you. I miss you even now as you lie next to me.

To look at you as you sleep, the color of your skin. How in the half-light of moon you cast your own light, as if you are all made of amber, Miliano. As if you are a little lantern, and everything in the house is golden too.

You used to be *tan chistoso. Muy bonachón, muy bromista.* Joking and singing off-key when you had your little drinks. *Tres vicios tengo y los tengo muy arraigados; de ser borracho, jugador, y enamorado . . .* Ay, my life, remember? Always *muy enamorado,* no? Are you still that boy I met at the San Lázaro country fair? Am I still that girl you kissed under the little avocado tree? It seems so far away from those days, Miliano.

We drag these bodies around with us, these bodies that have nothing at all to do with you, with me, with who we really are, these bodies that give us pleasure and pain. Though I've learned how to abandon mine at will, it seems to me we never free ourselves completely until we love, when we lose ourselves inside each other. Then we see a little of what is called heaven. When we can be that close that we no longer are Inés and Emiliano, but something bigger than our lives. And we can forgive, finally.

You and I, we've never been much for talking, have we? Poor thing, you don't know how to talk. Instead of talking with your lips, you put one leg around me when we sleep, to let me know it's all right. And we fall asleep like that, with one arm or a leg or one of those long monkey feet of yours touching mine. Your foot inside the hollow of my foot.

Does it surprise you I don't let go little things like that? There are so many things I don't forget even if I would do well to.

Inés, for the love I have for you. When my father pleaded, you can't imagine how I felt. How a pain entered my heart like a current of cold water and in that current were the days to come. But I said nothing.

Well then, my father said, *God help you. You've turned out just like the* perra *that bore you.* Then he turned around and I had no father.

I never felt so alone as that night. I gathered my things in my *rebozo* and ran out into the darkness to wait for you by the jacaranda tree. For a moment, all my courage left me. I wanted to turn around, call out, *'apá,* beg his forgiveness, and go back to sleeping on my *petate* against the cane-rush wall, waking before dawn to prepare the corn for the day's tortillas.

Perra. That word, the way my father spat it, as if in that one word I were betraying all the love he had given me all those years, as if he were closing all the doors to his heart.

Where could I hide from my father's anger? I could put out the eyes and stop the mouths of all the saints that wagged their tongues at me, but I could not stop my heart from hearing that word—*perra.* My father, my love, who would have nothing to do with me.

You don't like me to talk about my father, do you? I know, you and he never, well . . . Remember that thick scar across his left eyebrow? Kicked by a mule when he was a boy. Yes, that's how it happened. Tía Chucha said it was the reason he sometimes acted like a mule—but you're as stubborn as he was, aren't you, and no mule kicked you.

It's true, he never liked you. Since the days you started buying and selling livestock all through the *rancheritos.* By the time you were working the stables in Mexico City there was no mentioning your name. Because you'd never slept under a thatch roof, he said. Because you were a *charro,* and didn't wear the cotton whites of the *campesino.* Then he'd mutter, loud enough for me to hear, *That one doesn't know what it is to smell his own shit.*

I always thought you and he made such perfect enemies because you were so much alike. Except, unlike you, he was useless as a soldier. I never told you how the government forced him to enlist. Up in Guanajuato is where they sent him when you were busy with the Carrancistas, and Pancho Villa's boys were giving everyone a rough time up north. My father, who'd never been farther than

Amecameca, gray-haired and broken as he was, they took him. It was during the time the dead were piled up on the street corners like stones, when it wasn't safe for anyone, man or woman, to go out into the streets.

There was nothing to eat, Tía Chucha sick with the fever, and me taking care of us all. My father said better he should go to his brother Fulgencio's in Tenexcapán and see if they had corn there. *Take Malenita,* I said. *With a child they won't bother you.*

And so my father went out toward Tenexcapán dragging Malenita by the hand. But when night began to fall and they hadn't come back, well, imagine. It was the widow Elpidia who knocked on our door with Malenita howling and with the story they'd taken the men to the railroad station. *South to the work camps, or north to fight?* Tía Chucha asked. *If God wishes,* I said, *he'll be safe.*

That night Tía Chucha and I dreamt this dream. My father and my Tío Fulgencio standing against the back wall of the rice mill. *Who lives?* But they don't answer, afraid to give the wrong *viva. Shoot them; discuss politics later.*

At the moment the soldiers are about to fire, an officer, an acquaintance of my father's from before the war, rides by and orders them set free.

Then they took my father and my Tío Fulgencio to the train station, shuttled them into box cars with others, and didn't let them go until they reached Guanajuato where they were each given guns and orders to shoot at the Villistas.

With the fright of the firing squad and all, my father was never the same. In Guanajuato, he had to be sent to the military hospital, where he suffered a collapsed lung. They removed three of his ribs to cure him, and when he was finally well enough to travel, they sent him back to us.

All through the dry season my father lived on like that, with a hole in the back of his chest from which he breathed. Those days

I had to swab him with a sticky pitch pine and wrap him each morning in clean bandages. The opening oozed a spittle like the juice of the prickly pear, sticky and clear and with a smell both sweet and terrible like magnolia flowers rotting on the branch.

We did the best we could to nurse him, my Tía Chucha and I. Then one morning a *chachalaca* flew inside the house and battered against the ceiling. It took both of us with blankets and the broom to get it out. We didn't say anything but we thought about it for a long time.

Before the next new moon, I had a dream I was in church praying a rosary. But what I held between my hands wasn't my rosary with the glass beads, but one of human teeth. I let it drop, and the teeth bounced across the flagstones like pearls from a necklace. The dream and the bird were sign enough.

When my father called my mother's name one last time and died, the syllables came out sucked and coughed from that other mouth, like a drowned man's, and he expired finally in one last breath from that opening that killed him.

We buried him like that, with his three missing ribs wrapped in a handkerchief my mother had embroidered with his initials and with the hoofmark of the mule under his left eyebrow.

For eight days people arrived to pray the rosary. All the priests had long since fled, we had to pay a *rezandero* to say the last rites. Tía Chucha laid the cross of lime and sand, and set out flowers and a votive lamp, and on the ninth day, my *tía* raised the cross and called out my father's name—Remigio Alfaro—and my father's spirit flew away and left us.

But suppose he won't give us his permission.

That old goat, we'll be dead by the time he gives his permission. Better we just run off. He can't be angry forever.

Not even on his deathbed did he forgive you. I suppose you've never forgiven him either for calling in the authorities. I'm sure he only meant for them to scare you a little, to remind you of your obligations to me since I was expecting your child. Who could imagine they would force you to join the cavalry.

I can't make apologies on my father's behalf, but, well, what were we to think, Miliano? Those months you were gone, hiding out in Puebla because of the protest signatures, the political organizing, the work in the village defense. Me as big as a boat, Nicolás waiting to be born at any moment, and you nowhere to be found, and no money sent, and not a word. I was so young, I didn't know what else to do but abandon our house of stone and adobe and go back to my father's. Was I wrong to do that? You tell me.

I could endure my father's anger, but I was afraid for the child. I placed my hand on my belly and whispered—Child, be born when the moon is tender; even a tree must be pruned under the full moon so it will grow strong. And at the next full moon, I gave light, Tía Chucha holding up our handsome, strong-lunged boy.

Two planting seasons came and went, and we were preparing for the third when you came back from the cavalry and met your son for the first time. I thought you'd forgotten all about politics, and we could go on with our lives. But by the end of the year you were already behind the campaign to elect Patricio Leyva governor, as if all the troubles with the government, with my father, had meant nothing.

You gave me a pair of gold earrings as a wedding gift, remember? *I never said I'd marry you, Inés. Never.* Two filagree hoops with tiny flowers and fringe. I buried them when the government came, and went back for them later. But even these I had to sell when there was nothing to eat but boiled corn silk. They were the last things I sold.

Never. It made me feel a little crazy when you hurled that at me. That word with all its force.

But, Miliano, I thought . . .

You were foolish to have thought then.

That was years ago. We're all guilty of saying things we don't mean. *I never said . . .* I know. You don't want to hear it.

What am I to you now, Miliano? When you leave me? When you hesitate? Hover? The last time you gave a sigh that would fit into a spoon. What did you mean by that?

If I complain about these woman concerns of mine, I know you'll tell me—Inés, these aren't times for that—wait until later. But, Miliano, I'm tired of being told to wait.

Ay, you don't understand. Even if you had the words, you could never tell me. You don't know your own heart, men. Even when you are speaking with it in your hand.

I have my livestock, a little money my father left me. I'll set up a house for us in Cuautla of stone and adobe. We can live together, and later we'll see.

Nicolás is crazy about his two cows, La Fortuna *y* La Paloma. Because he's a man now, you said, when you gave him his birthday present. When you were thirteen, you were already buying and reselling animals throughout the ranches. To see if a beast is a good worker, you must tickle it on the back, no? If it can't bother itself to move, well then, it's lazy and won't be of any use. See, I've learned that much from you.

Remember the horse you found in Cuernavaca? Someone had hidden it in an upstairs bedroom, wild and spirited from being penned so long. She had poked her head from between the gold fringe of velvet drapery just as you rode by, just at that moment. A beauty like that making her appearance from a balcony like a woman waiting for her serenade. You laughed and joked about that and named her La Coquetona, remember? La Coquetona, yes.

When I met you at the country fair in San Lázaro, everyone knew you were the best man with horses in the state of Morelos. All the hacienda owners wanted you to work for them. Even as far as Mexico City. A *charro* among *charros*. The livestock, the horses bought and sold. Planting a bit when things were slow. Your brother Eufemio borrowing time and time again because he'd squandered every peso of his inheritance, but you've always prided yourself in being independent, no? You once confessed one of the happiest days of your life was the watermelon harvest that produced the 600 pesos.

And *my* happiest memory? The night I came to live with you, of course. I remember how your skin smelled sweet as the rind of a watermelon, like the fields after it has rained. I wanted my life to begin there, at that moment when I balanced that thin boy's body of yours on mine, as if you were made of balsa, as if you were boat and I river. The days to come, I thought, erasing the bitter sting of my father's good-bye.

There's been too much suffering, too much of our hearts hardening and drying like corpses. We've survived, eaten grass and corn cobs and rotten vegetables. And the epidemics have been as dangerous as the *federales*, the deserters, the bandits. Nine years.

In Cuautla it stank from so many dead. Nicolás would go out to play with the bullet shells he'd collected, or to watch the dead being buried in trenches. Once five federal corpses were piled up in the *zócalo*. We went through their pockets for money, jewelry, anything we could sell. When they burned the bodies, the fat ran off them in streams, and they jumped and wiggled as if they were trying to sit up. Nicolás had terrible dreams after that. I was too ashamed to tell him I did, too.

At first we couldn't bear to look at the bodies hanging in the trees. But after many months, you get used to them, curling and drying into leather in the sun day after day, dangling like earrings, so that they no longer terrify, they no longer mean anything. Perhaps that is worst of all.

Your sister tells me Nicolás takes after you these days, nervous and quick with words, like a sudden dust storm or shower of sparks. When you were away with the Seventh Cavalry, Tía Chucha and I would put smoke in Nicolás's mouth, so he would learn to talk early. All the other babies his age babbling like monkeys, but Nicolás always silent, always following us with those eyes all your kin have. Those are not Alfaro eyes, I remember my father saying.

The year you came back from the cavalry, you sent for us, me and the boy, and we lived in the house of stone and adobe. From your silences, I understood I was not to question our marriage. It was what it was. Nothing more. Wondering where you were the weeks I didn't see you, and why it was you arrived only for a few slender nights, always after nightfall and leaving before dawn. Our lives ran along as they had before. What good is it to have a husband and not have him? I thought.

When you began involving yourself with the Patricio Leyva campaign, we didn't see you for months at a time. Sometimes the boy and I would return to my father's house where I felt less alone. *Just for a few nights,* I said, unrolling a *petate* in my old corner against the cane-rush wall in the kitchen. *Until my husband returns.* But a few nights grew into weeks, and the weeks into months, until I spent more time under my father's thatch roof than in our house with the roof of tiles.

That's how the weeks and months passed. Your election to the town council. Your work defending the land titles. Then the parceling of the land when your name began to run all along the villages, up and down the Cuautla River. Zapata this and Zapata that. I couldn't go anywhere without hearing it. And each time, a kind of fear entered my heart like a cloud crossing the sun.

I spent the days chewing on this poison as I was grinding the corn, pretending to ignore what the other women washing at the river said. That you had several *pastimes*. That there was a certain María Josefa in Villa de Ayala. Then they would just laugh. It was worse for me those nights you did arrive and lay asleep next to me. I lay awake watching and watching you.

In the day, I could support the grief, wake up before dawn to prepare the day's tortillas, busy myself with the chores, the turkey hens, the planting and collecting of herbs. The boy already wearing his first pair of trousers and getting into all kinds of trouble when he wasn't being watched. There was enough to distract me in the day. But at night, you can't imagine.

Tía Chucha made me drink heart-flower tea—*yoloxochitl,* flower from the magnolia tree—petals soft and seamless as a tongue. *Yoloxochitl, flor de corazón,* with its breath of vanilla and honey. She prepared a tonic with the dried blossoms and applied a salve, mixed with the white of an egg, to the tender skin above my heart.

It was the season of rain. *Plum . . . plum plum.* All night I listened to that broken string of pearls, bead upon bead upon bead rolling across the waxy leaves of my heart.

I lived with that heartsickness inside me, Miliano, as if the days to come did not exist. And when it seemed the grief would not let me go, I wrapped one of your handkerchiefs around a dried hummingbird, went to the river, whispered, *Virgencita, ayúdame,* kissed it, then tossed the bundle into the waters where it disappeared for a moment before floating downstream in a dizzy swirl of foam.

That night, my heart circled and fluttered against my chest, and something beneath my eyelids palpitated so furiously, it wouldn't let me sleep. When I felt myself whirling against the beams of the house, I opened my eyes. I could see perfectly in the darkness. Beneath me—all of us asleep. Myself, there, in my *petate* against the kitchen wall, the boy asleep beside me. My father and my Tía Chucha sleeping in their corner of the house. Then I felt the room circle once, twice, until I found myself under the stars flying above the little avocado tree, above the house and the corral.

I passed the night in a delirious circle of sadness, of joy, reeling round and round above our roof of dried sugarcane leaves, the world as clear as if the noon sun shone. And when dawn arrived I flew back to my body that waited patiently for me where I'd left it, on the *petate* beside our Nicolás.

Each evening I flew a wider circle. And in the day, I withdrew further and further into myself, living only for those night flights. My father whispered to my Tía Chucha, *Ojos que no ven, corazón que no siente*. But my eyes did see and my heart suffered.

One night over *milpas* and beyond the *tlacolol*, over *barrancas* and thorny scrub forests, past the thatch roofs of the *jacales* and the stream where the women do the wash, beyond bright bougainvillea, high above canyons and across fields of rice and corn, I flew. The gawky stalks of banana trees swayed beneath me. I saw rivers of cold water and a river of water so bitter they say it flows from the sea. I didn't stop until I reached a grove of high laurels rustling in the center of a town square where all the whitewashed houses shone blue as abalone under the full moon. And I remember my wings were blue and soundless as the wings of a *tecolote*.

And when I alighted on the branch of a tamarind tree outside a window, I saw you asleep next to that woman from Villa de Ayala, that woman who is your wife sleeping beside you. And her skin shone blue in the moonlight and you were blue as well.

She wasn't at all like I'd imagined. I came up close and studied her hair. Nothing but an ordinary woman with her ordinary woman smell. She opened her mouth and gave a moan. And you pulled her close to you, Miliano. Then I felt a terrible grief inside me. The two of you asleep like that, your leg warm against hers, your foot inside the hollow of her foot.

They say I am the one who caused her children to die. From jealousy, from envy. What do you say? Her boy and girl both dead before they stopped sucking teat. She won't bear you any more children. But my boy, my girl are alive.

When a customer walks away after you've named your price, and then he comes back, that's when you raise your price. When you know you have what he wants. Something I learned from your horse-trading years.

You married her, that woman from Villa de Ayala, true. But see, you came back to me. You always come back. In between and beyond the others. That's my magic. You come back to me.

You visited me again Thursday last. I yanked you from the bed of that other one. I dreamt you, and when I awoke I was sure your spirit had just fluttered from the room. I have yanked you from your sleep before into the dream I was dreaming. Twisted you like a spiral of hair around a finger. Love, you arrived with your heart full of birds. And when you would not do my bidding and come when I commanded, I turned into the soul of a *tecolote* and kept vigil in the branches of a purple jacaranda outside your door to make sure no one would do my Miliano harm while he slept.

You sent a letter by messenger how many months afterward? On paper thin and crinkled as if it had been made with tears.

I burned copal in a clay bowl. Inhaled the smoke. Said a prayer in *mexicano* to the old gods, an Ave María in Spanish to La Virgen, and gave thanks. You were on your way home to us. The house of stone and adobe aired and swept clean, the night sweet with the scent of candles that had been burning continually since I saw you in the dream. Sometime after Nicolás had fallen asleep, the hoofbeats.

A silence between us like a language. When I held you, you trembled, a tree in rain. Ay, Miliano, I remember that, and it helps the days pass without bitterness.

What did you tell her about me? *That was before I knew you, Josefa. That chapter of my life with Inés Alfaro is finished.* But I'm a story that never ends. Pull one string and the whole cloth unravels.

Just before you came for Nicolás, he fell ill with the symptoms of the jealousy sickness, big boy that he was. But it was true, I was with child again. Malena was born without making a sound, because she remembered how she had been conceived—nights tangled around each other like smoke.

You and Villa were marching triumphantly down the streets of Mexico City, your hat filled with flowers the pretty girls tossed at you. The brim sagging under the weight like a basket.

I named our daughter after my mother. María Elena. Against my father's wishes.

You have your *pastimes*. That's how it's said, no? Your many *pastimes*. I know you take to your bed women half my age. Women the age of our Nicolás. You've left many mothers crying, as they say.

They say you have three women in Jojutla, all under one roof. And that your women treat each other with *a most extraordinary harmony, sisters in a cause who believe in the greater good of the revolution*. I say they can all go to hell, those newspaper journalists and the mothers who bore them. Did they ever ask me?

These stupid country girls, how can they resist you? The magnificent Zapata in his elegant *charro* costume, riding a splendid horse. Your wide sombrero a halo around your face. You're not a man for them; you're a legend, a myth, a god. But you are as well my husband. Albeit only sometimes.

How can a woman be happy in love? To love like this, to love as strong as we hate. That is how we are, the women of my family. We never forget a wrong. We know how to love and we know how to hate.

I've seen your other children in the dreams. María Luisa from that Gregoria Zúñiga in Quilamula after her twin sister Luz died on you childless. Diego born in Tlatizapán of that woman who calls herself *Missus* Jorge Piñeiro. Ana María in Cuautla from that she-goat Petra Torres. Mateo, son of that nobody, Jesusa Pérez of Temilpa. All your children born with those eyes of Zapata.

I know what I know. How you sleep cradled in my arms, how you love me with a pleasure close to sobbing, how I still the trembling in your chest and hold you, hold you, until those eyes look into mine.

Your eyes. Ay! Your eyes. Eyes with teeth. Terrible as obsidian. The days to come in those eyes, *el porvenir,* the days gone by. And beneath that fierceness, something ancient and tender as rain.

Miliano, Milianito. And I sing you that song I sang Nicolás and Malenita when they were little and would not sleep.

Seasons of war, a little half-peace now and then, and then war and war again. Running up to the hills when the *federales* come, coming back down when they've gone.

Before the war, it was the *caciques* who were after the young girls and the married women. They had their hands on everything it seems—the land, law, women. Remember when they found that *desgraciado* Policarpo Cisneros in the arms of the Quintero girl? *¡Virgen purísima!* She was only a little thing of twelve years. And he, what? At least eighty, I imagine.

Desgraciados. All members of one army against us, no? The *federales,* the *caciques,* one as bad as the other, stealing our hens, stealing the women at night. What long sharp howls the women would let go when they carried them off. The next morning the women would be back, and we would say *Buenos días,* as if nothing had happened.

Since the war began, we've gotten used to sleeping in the corral.

Or in the hills, in trees, in caves with the spiders and scorpions. We hide ourselves as best we can when the *federales* arrive, behind rocks or in *barrancas,* or in the pine and tall grass when there is nothing else to hide behind. Sometimes I build a shelter for us with cane branches in the mountains. Sometimes the people of the cold lands give us boiled water sweetened with cane sugar, and we stay until we can gather a little strength, until the sun has warmed our bones and it is safe to come back down.

Before the war, when Tía Chucha was alive, we passed the days selling at all the town markets—chickens, turkey hens, cloth, coffee, the herbs we collected in the hills or grew in the garden. That's how our weeks and months came and went.

I sold bread and candles. I planted corn and beans back then and harvested coffee at times too. I've sold all kinds of things. I even know how to buy and resell animals. And now I know how to work the *tlacolol,* which is the worst of all—your hands and feet split and swollen from the machete and hoe.

Sometimes I find sweet potatoes in the abandoned fields, or squash, or corn. And this we eat raw, too tired, too hungry to cook anything. We've eaten like the birds, what we could pluck from the trees—guava, mango, tamarind, almond when in season. We've gone without corn for the tortillas, made do when there were no kernels to be had, eaten the cobs as well as the flower.

My *metate*, my good shawl, my fancy *huipil*, my filigree earrings, anything I could sell, I've sold. The corn sells for one peso and a half a *cuartillo* when one can find a handful. I soak and boil and grind it without even letting it cool, a few tortillas to feed Malenita, who is always hungry, and if there is anything left, I feed myself.

Tía Chucha caught the sickness of the wind in the hot country. I used all her remedies and my own, *guacamaya* feathers, eggs, cocoa beans, chamomile oil, rosemary, but there was no help for her. I thought I would finish myself crying, all my mother's people gone from me, but there was the girl to think about. Nothing to do but go on, *aguantar,* until I could let go that grief. Ay, how terrible those times.

I go on surviving, hiding, searching if only for Malenita's sake. Our little plantings, that's how we get along. The government run off with the *maíz,* the chickens, my prize turkey hens and rabbits. Everyone has had his turn to do us harm.

Now I'm going to tell you about when they burned the house, the one you bought for us. I was sick with the fever. Headache and a terrible pain in the back of my calves. Fleas, babies crying, gunshots in the distance, someone crying out *el gobierno,* a gallop of horses in my head, and the shouting of those going off to join troops and of those staying. I could barely manage to drag myself up the hills. Malenita was suffering one of her *corajes* and refused to walk, sucking the collar of her blouse and crying. I had to carry her on my back with her little feet kicking me all the way until I gave her half of a hard tortilla to eat and she forgot about her anger and fell asleep. By the time the sun was strong and we were far away enough to feel safe, I was weak. I slept without dreaming, holding Malenita's cool body against my burning. When I woke the world was filled with stars, and the stars carried me back to the village and showed me.

It was like this. The village did not look like our village. The trees, the mountains against the sky, the land, yes, that was still as we remembered it, but the village was no longer a village. Everything pocked and in ruins. Our house with its roof tiles gone. The walls blistered and black. Pots, pans, jugs, dishes axed into shards, our shawls and blankets torn and trampled. The seed we had left, what we'd saved and stored that year, scattered, the birds enjoying it.

Hens, cows, pigs, goats, rabbits, all slaughtered. Not even the dogs were spared and were strung from the trees. The Carrancistas destroyed everything, because, as they say, *Even the stones here are Zapatistas*. And what was not destroyed was carried off by their women, who descended behind them like a plague of vultures to pick us clean.

It's *her* fault, the villagers said when they returned. *Nagual. Bruja*. Then I understood how alone I was.

Miliano, what I'm about to say to you now, only to you do I tell it, to no one else have I confessed it. It's necessary I say it; I won't rest until I undo it from my heart.

They say when I was a child I caused a hailstorm that ruined the new corn. When I was so young I don't even remember. In Tetelcingo that's what they say.

That's why the years the harvest was bad and the times especially hard, they wanted to burn me with green wood. It was my mother they killed instead, but not with green wood. When they delivered her to our door, I cried until I finished myself crying. I was sick, sick, for several days, and they say I vomited worms, but I don't remember that. Only the terrible dreams I suffered during the fever.

My Tía Chucha cured me with branches from the pepper tree and with the broom. And for a long time afterward, my legs felt as if they were stuffed with rags, and I kept seeing little purple stars winking and whirling just out of reach.

It wasn't until I was well enough to go outside again that I noticed the crosses of pressed *pericón* flowers on all the village doorways and in the *milpa* too. From then on the villagers avoided me, as if they meant to punish me by not talking, just as they'd punished my mother with those words that thumped and thudded like the hail that killed the corn.

That's why we had to move the seven kilometers from Tetelcingo to Cuautla, as if we were from that village and not the other, and that's how it was we came to live with my Tía Chucha, little by little taking my mother's place as my teacher, and later as my father's wife.

My Tía Chucha, she was the one who taught me to use my sight, just as her mother had taught her. The women in my family, we've always had the power to see with more than our eyes. My mother, my Tía Chucha, me. Our Malenita as well.

It's only now when they murmur *bruja, nagual,* behind my back, just as they hurled those words at my mother, that I realize how alike my mother and I are. How words can hold their own magic. How a word can charm, and how a word can kill. This I've understood.

Mujeriego. I dislike the word. Why not *hombreriega?* Why not? The word loses its luster. *Hombreriega*. Is that what I am? My mother? But in the mouth of men, the word is flint-edged and heavy, makes a drum of the body, something to maim and bruise, and sometimes kill.

What is it I am to you? Sometime wife? Lover? Whore? Which? To be one is not so terrible as being all.

I've needed to hear it from you. To verify what I've always thought I knew. You'll say I've grown crazy from living on dried grass and corn silk. But I swear I've never seen more clearly than these days.

Ay, Miliano, don't you see? The wars begin here, in our hearts and in our beds. You have a daughter. How do you want her treated? Like you treated me?

All I've wanted was words, that magic to soothe me a little, what you could not give me.

The months I disappeared, I don't think you understood my reasons. I assumed I made no difference to you. Only Nicolás mattered. And that's when you took him from me.

When Nicolás lost his last milk tooth, you sent for him, left him in your sister's care. He's lived like deer in the mountains, sometimes following you, sometimes meeting you ahead of your campaigns, always within reach. I know. I let him go. I agreed, yes, because a boy should be with his father, I said. But the truth is I wanted a part of me always hovering near you. How hard it must be for you to keep letting Nicolás go. And yet, he is always yours. Always.

When the *federales* captured Nicolás and took him to Tepaltzingo, you arrived with him asleep in your arms after your brother and Chico Franco rescued him. If anything happens to this child, you said, if anything . . . and started to cry. I didn't say anything, Miliano, but you can't imagine how in that instant, I wanted to be small and fit inside your heart, I wanted to belong to you like the boy, and know you loved me.

If I am a witch, then so be it, I said. And I took to eating black things—*huitlacoche* the corn mushroom, coffee, dark chiles, the bruised part of fruit, the darkest, blackest things to make me hard and strong.

You rarely talk. Your voice, Miliano, thin and light as a woman's, almost delicate. Your way of talking is sudden, quick, like water leaping. And yet I know what that voice of yours is capable of.

I remember after the massacre of Tlatizapán, 286 men and women and children slaughtered by the Carrancistas. Your thin figure, haggard and drawn, your face small and dark under your wide sombrero. I remember even your horse looked half-starved and wild that dusty, hot June day.

It was as if misery laughed at us. Even the sky was sad, the light leaden and dull, the air sticky and everything covered with flies. Women filled the streets searching among the corpses for their dead.

Everyone was tired, exhausted from running from the Carrancistas. The government had chased us almost as far as Jojutla. But you spoke in *mexicano*, you spoke to us in our language, with your heart in your hand, Miliano, which is why we listened to you. The people were tired, but they listened. Tired of surviving, of living, of enduring. Many were deserting and going back to their villages. *If you don't want to fight anymore*, you said, *we'll all go to the devil. What do you mean you are tired? When you elected me, I said I would represent you if you backed me. But now you must back me, I've kept my word. You wanted a man who wore pants, and I've been that man. And now, if you don't mean to fight, well then, there's nothing I can do.*

We were filthy, exhausted, hungry, but we followed you.

Under the little avocado tree behind my father's house is where you first kissed me. A crooked kiss, all wrong, on the side of the mouth. *You belong to me now,* you said, and I did.

The way you rode in the morning of the San Lázaro fair on a pretty horse as dark as your eyes. The sky was sorrel-colored, remember? Everything swelled and smelled of rain. A cool shadow fell across the village. You were dressed all in black as is your custom. A graceful, elegant man, thin and tall.

You wore a short black linen *charro* jacket, black trousers of cashmere adorned with silver buttons, and a lavender shirt knotted at the collar with a blue silk neckerchief. Your sombrero had a horsehair braid and tassel and a border of carnations embroidered along the wide brim in gold and silver threads. You wore the sombrero set forward—not at the back of the head as others do—so it would shade those eyes of yours, those eyes that watched and waited. Even then I knew it was an animal to match mine.

Suppose my father won't let me?

We'll run off, he can't be angry for always.

Wait until the end of the harvest.

You pulled me toward you under the little avocado tree and kissed me. A kiss tasting of warm beer and whiskers. *You belong to me now.*

It was during the plum season we met. I saw you at the country fair at San Lázaro. I wore my braids up away from the neck with bright ribbons. My hair freshly washed and combed with oil prepared with the ground bone of the mamey. And the neckline of my *huipil,* a white one, I remember, showed off my neck and collarbones.

You were riding a fine horse, silver-saddled with a fringe of red and black silk tassels, and your hands, beautiful hands, long and sensitive, rested lightly on the reins. I was afraid of you at first, but I didn't show it. How pretty you made your horse prance.

You circled when I tried to cross the *zócalo,* I remember. I pretended not to see you until you rode your horse in my path, and I tried to dodge one way, then the other, like a calf in a *jaripeo.* I could hear the laughter of your friends from under the shadows of the arcades. And when it was clear there was no avoiding you, I looked up at you and said, *With your permission.* You did not insist, you touched the brim of your hat, and let me go, and I heard your friend Francisco Franco, the one I would later know as Chico, say, *Small, but bigger than you, Miliano.*

So is it yes? I didn't know what to say, I was still so little, just laughed, and you kissed me like that, on my teeth.

Yes? and pressed me against the avocado tree. *No, is it?* And I said yes, then I said no, and yes, your kisses arriving in between.

Love? We don't say that word. For you it has to do with stroking with your eyes what catches your fancy, then lassoing and harnessing and corraling. Yanking home what is easy to take.

But not for me. Not from the start. You were handsome, yes, but I didn't like handsome men, thinking they could have whomever they wanted. I wanted to be, then, the one you could not have. I didn't lower my eyes like the other girls when I felt you looking at me.

I'll set up a house for us. We can live together, and later we'll see.

But suppose one day you leave me.

Never.

Wait at least until the end of the harvest.

I remember how your skin burned to the touch. How you smelled of lemongrass and smoke. I balanced that thin boy's body of yours on mine.

Something undid itself—gently, like a braid of hair unraveling. And I said, *Ay, mi chulito, mi chulito, mi chulito*, over and over.

Mornings and nights I think your scent is still in the blankets, wake remembering you are tangled somewhere between the sleeping and the waking. The scent of your skin, the mole above the broom of your thick mustache, how you fit in my hands.

Would it be right to tell you, each night you sleep here, after your cognac and cigar, when I'm certain you are finally sleeping, I sniff your skin. Your fingers sweet with the scent of tobacco. The fluted collarbones, the purple knot of the nipple, the deep, plum color of your sex, the thin legs and long, thin feet.

I examine at my leisure your black trousers with the silver buttons, the lovely shirt, the embroidered sombrero, the fine braid stitching on the border of your *charro* jacket, admire the workmanship, the spurs, leggings, the handsome black boots.

And when you are gone, I re-create you from memory. Rub warmth into your fingertips. Take that dimpled chin of yours between my teeth. All the parts are there except your belly. I want to rub my face in its color, say no, no, no. Ay. Feel its warmth from my left cheek to the right. Run my tongue from the hollow in your throat, between the smooth stones of your chest, across the trail of down below the navel, lose myself in the dark scent of your sex. To look at you as you sleep, the color of your skin. How in the half-light of moon you cast your own light, as if you are a man made of amber.

Are you my general? Or only my Milianito? I think, I don't know what you say, you don't belong to me nor to that woman from Villa de Ayala. You don't belong to anyone, no? Except the land. *La madre tierra que nos mantiene y cuida.* Every one of us.

I rise high and higher, the house shutting itself like an eye. I fly farther than I've ever flown before, farther than the clouds, farther than our Lord Sun, husband of the moon. Till all at once I look beneath me and see our lives, clear and still, far away and near.

And I see our future and our past, Miliano, one single thread already lived and nothing to be done about it. And I see the face of the man who will betray you. The place and the hour. The gift of a horse the color of gold dust. A breakfast of warm beer swirling in your belly. The hacienda gates opening. The pretty bugles doing the honors. *TirriLEE tirREE.* Bullets like a sudden shower of stones. And in that instant, a feeling of relief almost. And loneliness, just like that other loneliness of being born.

And I see my clean *huipil* and my silk Sunday shawl. My rosary placed between my hands and a palm cross that has been blessed. Eight days people arriving to pray. And on the ninth day, the cross of lime and sand raised, and my name called out—Inés Alfaro. The twisted neck of a rooster. Pork tamales wrapped in corn leaves. The masqueraders dancing, the men dressed as women, the women as men. Violins, guitars, one loud drum.

And I see other faces and other lives. My mother in a field of cempoaxúchitl flowers with a man who is not my father. Her *rebozo de bolita* spread beneath them. The smell of crushed grass and garlic. How, at a signal from her lover, the others descend. The clouds scurrying away. A machete-sharp cane stake greased with lard and driven into the earth. How the men gather my mother like a bundle of corn. Her sharp cry against the infinity of sky when the cane stake pierces her. How each waiting his turn grunts words like hail that splits open the skin, just as before they'd whispered words of love.

The star of her sex open to the sky. Clouds moving soundlessly, and the sky changing colors. Hours. Eyes still fixed on the clouds the morning they find her—braids undone, a man's sombrero tipped on her head, a cigar in her mouth, as if to say, this is what we do to women who try to act like men.

The small black bundle that is my mother delivered to my father's door. My father without a "who" or "how." He knows as well as everyone.

How the sky let go a storm of stones. The corn harvest ruined. And how we move from Tetelcingo to my Tía Chucha's in Cuautla.

And I see our children. Malenita with her twins, who will never marry, two brave *solteronas* living out their lives selling herbs in La Merced in Mexico City.

And our Nicolás, a grown man, the grief and shame Nicolás will bring to the Zapata name when he kicks up a fuss about the parcel of land the government gives him, how it isn't enough, how it's never enough, how the son of a great man should not live like a peasant. The older Anenecuilcans shaking their heads when he sells the Zapata name to the PRI campaign.

And I see the ancient land titles the smoky morning they are drawn up in Náhuatl and recorded on tree-bark paper—*conceded to our pueblo the 25th of September of 1607 by the Viceroy of New Spain*—the land grants that prove the land has always been our land.

And I see that dappled afternoon in Anenecuilco when the government has begun to look for you. And I see you unearth the strong box buried under the main altar of the village church, and hand it to Chico Franco—*If you lose this, I'll have you dangling from the tallest tree*, compadre. *Not before they fill me with bullets,* Chico said and laughed.

And the evening, already as an old man, in the Canyon of the Wolves, Chico Franco running and running, old wolf, old cunning, the government men Nicolás sent shouting behind him, his sons Vírulo and Julián, young, crumpled on the cool courtyard tiles like bougainvillea blossoms, and how useless it all is, because the deeds are buried under the floorboards of a *pulquería* named La Providencia, and no one knowing where they are after the bullets pierce Chico's body. Nothing better or worse than before, and nothing the same or different.

And I see rivers of stars and the wide sea with its sad voice, and emerald fish fluttering on the sea bottom, glad to be themselves. And bell towers and blue forests, and a store window filled with hats. A burnt foot like the inside of a plum. A lice comb with two nits. The lace hem of a woman's dress. The violet smoke from a cigarette. A boy urinating into a tin. The milky eyes of a blind man. The chipped finger of a San Isidro statue. The tawny bellies of dark women giving life.

And more lives and more blood, those being born as well as those dying, the ones who ask questions and the ones who keep quiet, the days of grief and all the flower colors of joy.

Ay papacito, cielito de mi corazón, now the burros are complaining. The rooster beginning his cries. Morning already? Wait, I want to remember everything before you leave me.

How you looked at me in the San Lázaro plaza. How you kissed me under my father's avocado tree. Nights you loved me with a pleasure close to sobbing, how I stilled the trembling in your chest and held you, held you. Miliano, Milianito.

My sky, my life, my eyes. Let me look at you. Before you open those eyes of yours. The days to come, the days gone by. Before we go back to what we'll always be.

Anguiano Religious Articles Rosaries Statues Medals Incense Candles Talismans Perfumes Oils Herbs

You know that religious store on Soledad across from Sanitary Tortillas? Next to El Divorcio Lounge. Don't go in there. The man who owns it is a crab ass. I'm not the only one who says it. He's famous for being a crab ass.

I know all about him, but I stopped in anyway. Because I needed a Virgen de Guadalupe and the Preciado sisters on South Laredo didn't have nothing that didn't look as if someone made it with their feet.

A statue is what I was thinking, or maybe those pretty 3-D pictures, the ones made from strips of cardboard that you look at sideways and you see the Santo Niño de Atocha, and you look at it straight and it's La Virgen, and you look at it from the other side and it's Saint Lucy with her eyes on a plate or maybe San Martín Caballero cutting his Roman cape in half with a sword and giving it to a beggar, only I want to know how come he didn't give that beggar *all* of his cape if he's so saintly, right?

Well, that's what I was looking for. One of those framed pictures with a silver strip of aluminum foil on the bottom and top, the wooden frame painted a happy pink or turquoise. You can buy them cheaper on the other side, but I didn't have time to go to Nuevo

Laredo 'cause I only found out about Tencha Tuesday. They put her right in Santa Rosa Hospital. I had to take a half-day off work and the bus, well, what was I going to do? It's either Anguiano Religious Articles or Sisters Preciado Botánica.

Then after I walk all the way from Santa Rosa in the heat, guess what? Anguiano's is closed even though I could see him sitting in there in the dark. I'm knocking and knocking, knocking and knocking on the glass with a quarter. Know what he does before unlocking? Looks me up and down like if I'm one of those ladies from the Cactus Hotel or the Court House Pawnshop or the Western Wear come to rob him.

I was thinking about those framed holy pictures with glitter in the window. But then I saw some Virgen de Guadalupe statues with real hair eyelashes. Well, not real hair, but some stiff black stuff like brushes, only I didn't like how La Virgen looked with furry eyelashes—*bien* mean, like *los amores de la calle*. That's not right.

I looked at all the Virgen de Guadalupes he had. The statues, the framed pictures, the holy cards, and candles. Because I only got $10. And by then, there was other people had come in. But you know what he says to me—you won't believe it—he says, I can see you're not going to buy anything. Loud and in Spanish. I can see you're not going to buy anything.

Oh, but I am, I says, I just need a little more time to think.

Well, if it's thinking you want, you just go across the street to the church to think—you're just wasting my time and yours thinking here.

Honest to God. Real ugly is how he talked to me. Well, go across the street to San Fernando if you want to think—you're just wasting my time and yours thinking here.

I should've told him, You go to hell. But what for? He's already headed there.

Little Miracles, Kept Promises

Exvoto Donated as Promised

On the 20th of December of 1988 we suffered a terrible disaster on the road to Corpus Christi. The bus we were riding skidded and overturned near Robstown and a lady and her little girl were killed. Thanks to La Virgen de Guadalupe we are alive, all of us miraculously unharmed, and with no visible scars, except we are afraid to ride buses. We dedicate this retablo to La Virgencita with our affection and gratitude and our everlasting faith.

Familia Arteaga
Alice, Texas
G.R. (Gracias Recibido/Thanks Given)

Blessed Santo Niño de Atocha,

Thank you for helping us when Chapa's truck got stolen. We didn't know how we was going to make it. He needs it to get to work, and this job, well, he's been on probation since we got him to quit drinking. Raquel and the kids are hardly ever afraid of him anymore, and we are proud parents. We don't know how we can repay you for everything you have done for our family. We will light a candle to you every Sunday and never forget you.

Sidronio Tijerina
Brenda A. Camacho de Tijerina
San Angelo, Texas

Dear San Martín de Porres,

Please send us clothes, furniture, shoes, dishes. We need anything that don't eat. Since the fire we have to start all over again and Lalo's disability check ain't much and don't go far. Zulema would like to finish school but I says she can just forget about it now. She's our oldest and her place is at home helping us out I told her. Please make her see some sense. She's all we got.

Thanking you,
Adelfa Vásquez
Escobas, Texas

Dear San Antonio de Padua,

Can you please help me find a man who isn't a pain in the nalgas. There aren't any in Texas, I swear. Especially not in San Antonio.

Can you do something about all the educated Chicanos who have to go to California to find a job. I guess what my sister Irma says is true: "If you didn't get a husband when you were in college, you don't get one."

I would appreciate it very much if you sent me a man who speaks Spanish, who at least can pronounce his name the way it's supposed to be pronounced. Someone please who never calls himself "Hispanic" unless he's applying for a grant from Washington, D.C.

Can you send me a man man. I mean someone who's not ashamed to be seen cooking or cleaning or looking after himself. In other words, a man who acts like an adult. Not one who's never lived alone, never bought his own underwear, never ironed his own shirts, never even heated his own tortillas. In other words, don't send me someone like my brothers who my mother ruined with too much chichi, or I'll throw him back.

I'll turn your statue upside down until you send him to me. I've put up with too much too long, and now I'm just too intelligent, too powerful, too beautiful, too sure of who I am finally to deserve anything less.

Ms. Barbara Ybañez
San Antonio, TX

Dear Niño Fidencio,

I would like for you to help me get a job with good pay, benefits, and retirement plan. I promise you if you help me I will make a pilgrimage to your tomb in Espinazo and bring you flowers. Many thanks.

César Escandón
Pharr, Tejas

DEAR DON PEDRITO JARAMILLO HEALER OF LOS OLMOS

MY NAME IS ENRIQUETA ANTONIA SANDOVAL I LIVE IN SAN MARCOS TX I AM SICK THEY OPERATED ME FROM A KIDNEY AND A TUMOR OF CANCER BUT THANKS TO GOD I AM ALIVE BUT I HAVE TO GET TREATMENTS FOR A YEAR THE KIMO I AM 2½ YEARS OLD BUT MY GRANDMA BROUGHT ME THAT YOU AND OUR LORD WHO IS IN THE HEAVENS WILL CURE ME WITH THIS LETTER THAT I AM DEPOSITING HERE ITS MY GRANDMA WHO IS WRITING THIS I HOPE EVERYBODY WHO SEES THIS LETTER WILL TAKE A MINUTE TO ASK FOR MY HEALTH

ENRIQUETA ANTONIA SANDOVAL
2 AND A HALF YEARS OLD

I LEOCADIA DIMAS VDA. DE CORDERO OF SAN MARCOS TX HAVE COME TO PAY THIS REQUEST TO DON PEDRITO THAT MY GRANDDAUGHTER WILL COME OUT FINE FROM HER OPERATION

THANKS TO GOD AND THOSE WHO HELPED SUCH GOOD DOCTORS THAT DID THEIR JOB WELL THE REST IS IN GODS HANDS THAT HE DO HIS WILL MANY THANKS WITH ALL MY HEART.

YOUR VERY RESPECTFUL SERVANT
LEOCADIA

Oh Mighty Poderosos, Blessed Powerful Ones,

You who are crowned in heaven and who are so close to our Divine Savior, I implore your intercession before the Almighty on my behalf. I ask for peace of spirit and prosperity, and that the demons in my path that are the cause of all my woes be removed so that they no longer torment me. Look favorably on this petition and bless me, that I may continue to glorify your deeds with all my heart—santísimo Niño Fidencio, gran General Pancho Villa, bendito Don Pedrito Jaramillo, virtuoso John F. Kennedy, and blessed Pope John Paul. Amen.

Gertrudis Parra
Uvalde, Tejas

Father Almighty,

Teach me to love my husband again. Forgive me.

s.
Corpus Christi

Seven African Powers that surround our Savior—Obatala, Yemaya, Ochún, Orunla, Ogun, Elegua, and Shango—why don't you behave and be good to me? Oh Seven African Powers, come on, don't be bad. Let my Illinois lottery ticket win, and if it does, don't let my cousin Cirilo in Chicago cheat me out of my winnings, since I'm the one who pays for the ticket and all he does is buy it for me each week—if he does even that. He's my cousin, but like the Bible says, better to say nothing than to say nothing nice.

Protect me from the evil eye of the envious and don't let my enemies do me harm, because I've never done a thing wrong to anyone first. Save this good Christian who the wicked have taken advantage of.

Seven Powers, reward my devotion with good luck. Look after me, why don't you? And don't forget me because I never forget you.

Moises Ildefonso Mata
San Antonio, Texas

Virgencita de Guadalupe,

I promise to walk to your shrine on my knees the very first day I get back, I swear, if you will only get the Tortillería la Casa de la Masa to pay me the $253.72 they owe me for two weeks' work. I put in 67½ hours that first week and 79 hours the second, and I don't have anything to show for it yet. I calculated with the taxes deducted, I have $253.72 coming to me. That's all I'm asking for. The $253.72 I have coming to me.

I have asked the proprietors Blanquita and Rudy Mondragón, and they keep telling me next week, next week, next week. And it's almost the middle of the third week already and I don't know how I'm going to do it to pay this week's rent, since I'm already behind, and the other guys have loaned me as much as they're able, and I don't know what I'm going to do, I don't know what I'm going to do.

My wife and the kids and my in-laws all depend on what I send home. We are humble people, Virgencita. You know I'm not full of vices. That's how I am. It's been hard for me to live here so far away without seeing my wife, you know. And sometimes one gets tempted, but no, and no, and no. I'm not like that. Please, Virgencita, all I'm asking for is my $253.72. There is no one else I can turn to here in this country, and well, if you can't help me, well, I just don't know.

Arnulfo Contreras
San Antonio, Tejas

Saint Sebastian who was persecuted with arrows and then survived, thank you for answering my prayers! All them arrows that had persecuted me—my brother-in-law Ernie and my sister Alba and their kids—el Junior, la Gloria, and el Skyler—all gone. And now my home sweet home is mine again, and my Dianita bien lovey-dovey, and my kids got something to say to me besides who hit who.

Here is the little gold milagrito I promised you, a little house, see? And it ain't that cheap gold-plate shit either. So now that I paid you back, we're even, right? Cause I don't like for no one to say Victor Lozano don't pay his debts. I pays cash on the line, bro. And Victor Lozano's word like his deeds is solid gold.

Victor A. Lozano
Houston, TX

Dear San Lázaro,

My mother's comadre Demetria said if I prayed to you that like maybe you could help me because you were raised from the dead and did a lot of miracles and maybe if I lit a candle every night for seven days and prayed, you might maybe could help me with my face breaking out with so many pimples. Thank you.

Rubén Ledesma
Hebbronville, Texas

Santísima Señora de San Juan de los Lagos,

We came to see you twice when they brought you to San Antonio, my mother and my sister Yolanda and two of my aunts, Tía Enedina and my Tía Perla, and we drove all the way from Beeville just to visit you and make our requests.

I don't know what my Tía Enedina asked for, she's always so secretive, but probably it had to do with her son Beto who doesn't do anything but hang around the house and get into trouble. And my Tía Perla no doubt complained about her ladies' problems—her ovaries that itch, her tangled fallopians, her uterus that makes her seasick with all its flipping and flopping. And Mami who said she only came along for the ride, lit three candles so you would bless us all and sweep jealousy and bitterness from our hearts because that's what she says every day and every night. And my sister Yoli asked that you help her lose weight because I don't want to wind up like Tía Perla, embroidering altar cloths and dressing saints.

But that was a year ago, Virgencita, and since then my cousin Beto was fined for killing the neighbor's rooster with a flying Big Red bottle, and my Tía Perla is convinced her uterus has fallen because when she walks something inside her rattles like a maraca, and my mother and my aunts are arguing and yelling at each other same as always. And my stupid sister Yoli is still sending away for even stupider products like the Grasa Fantástica, guaranteed to burn away fat—It really works, Tere, just rub some on while you're watching TV—only she's fatter than ever and just as sad.

What I realize is that we all made the trip to San Antonio to ask something of you, Virgencita, we all needed you to listen to us. And of all of us, my mama and sister Yoli, and my aunts Enedina and Perla, of all of us, you granted me my petition and sent, just like I asked, a guy who would love only me because I was tired of looking at girls younger than me walking along the street or riding in cars or standing in front of the school with a guy's arm hooked around their neck.

So what is it I'm asking for? Please, Virgencita. Lift this heavy cross from my shoulders and leave me like I was before, wind on my neck, my arms swinging free, and no one telling me how I ought to be.

Teresa Galindo
Beeville, Texas

Miraculous Black Christ of Esquipulas,

Please make our grandson to be nice to us and stay away from drugs. Save him to find a job and move away from us. Thank you.

Grandma y Grandfather
Harlingen

M3r1c5l45s Bl1ck Chr3st 4f 2sq53p5l1s,

3 1sk y45, L4rd, w3th 1ll my h21rt pl21s2 w1tch 4v2r M1nny B2n1v3d2s wh4 3s 4v2rs21s. 3 l4v2 h3m 1nd 3 d4n't

kn4w wh1t t4 d4 1b45t 1ll th3s l4v2 s1dn2ss 1nd sh1m2 th1t f3lls m2.

B2nj1m3n T.
D21 R34 TX

Milagroso Cristo Negro de Esquipulas,

Te ofrezco este retrato de mis niños. Wáchelos, Dios Santo, y si le quitas el trago a mi hijo te prometo prender velitas. Ayúdanos con nuestras cuentas, Señor, y que el cheque del income tax nos llegue pronto para pagar los biles. Danos una buena vida y que les ayudes a mis hijos a cambiar sus modos. Tú que eres tan bondadoso escucha estas peticiones que te pido con todo mi corazón y con toda la fe de mi alma. Ten piedad, Padre mio. Mi nombre es Adela O.

Elizondo.
Cotulla TX

Milagroso Cristo Negro,

Thank you por el milagro de haber graduado de high school. Aquí le regalo mi retrato de graduation.

Fito Moroles
Rockport, Texas

Cristo Negro,

Venimos desde muy lejos. Infinitas gracias, Señor. Gracias por habernos escuchado.

Familia Armendáriz G.
Matamoros, Tamps. México

Jesus Christ,

Please keep Deborah Abrego and Ralph S. Urrea together forever.

Love,
Deborah Abrego
Sabinal, Texas

Blessed Virgen de los Remedios,

Señora Dolores Alcalá de Corchado finds herself gravely ill from a complication that resulted after a delicate operation she underwent Thursday last, and from which she was recovering satisfactorily until suffering a hemmorhage Tuesday morning. Please intercede on her behalf. We leave her in the hands of God, that His will be done, now that we have witnessed her suffering and don't know whether she should die or continue this life. Her husband of forty-eight years offers this request with all his heart.

Señor Gustavo Corchado B.
Laredo, Tejas

Madrecita de Dios,

Thank you. Our child is born healthy!

Rene y Janie Garza
Hondo, TX

Saint Jude, patron saint of lost causes,

Help me pass my English 320, British Restoration Literature class and everything to turn out ok.

Eliberto González
Dallas

Virgencita . . .

I've cut off my hair just like I promised I would and pinned my braid here by your statue. Above a Toys "Я" Us name tag that says IZAURA. Along several hospital bracelets. Next to a business card for Sergio's Casa de la Belleza Beauty College. Domingo Reyna's driver's license. Notes printed on the flaps of envelopes. Silk roses, plastic roses, paper roses, roses crocheted out of fluorescent orange yarn. Photo button of a baby in a *charro* hat. Caramel-skinned woman in a white graduation cap and gown. Mean dude in bandanna and tattoos. Oval black-and-white passport portrait of the sad uncle who never married. A mama in a sleeveless dress watering the porch plants. Sweet boy with new mustache and new soldier uniform. Teenager with a little bit of herself sitting on her lap. Blurred husband and wife leaning one into the other as if joined at the hip. Black-and-white photo of the cousins *la* Josie *y la* Mary Helen, circa 1942. Polaroid of Sylvia Rios, First Holy Communion, age nine years.

So many *milagritos* safety-pinned here, so many little miracles dangling from red thread—a gold Sacred Heart, a tiny copper arm, a kneeling man in silver, a bottle, a brass truck, a foot, a house, a hand, a baby, a cat, a breast, a tooth, a belly button, an evil eye. So many petitions, so many promises made and kept. And there is nothing I can give you except this braid of hair the color of coffee in a glass.

Chayo, what have you done! All that beautiful hair.

Chayito, how could you ruin in one second what your mother took years to create?

You might as well've plucked out your eyes like Saint Lucy. All that hair!

My mother cried, did I tell you? All that beautiful hair . . .

I've cut off my hair. Which I've never cut since the day I was born. The donkey tail in a birthday game. Something shed like a snakeskin.

My head as light as if I'd raised it from water. My heart buoyant again, as if before I'd worn *el* Sagrado Corazón in my open chest. I could've lit this entire church with my grief.

I'm a bell without a clapper. A woman with one foot in this world and one foot in that. A woman straddling both. This thing between my legs, this unmentionable.

I'm a snake swallowing its tail. I'm my history and my future. All my ancestors' ancestors inside my own belly. All my futures and all my pasts.

I've had to steel and hoard and hone myself. I've had to push the furniture against the door and not let you in.

What you doing sitting in there in the dark?

I'm thinking.

Thinking of what?

Just . . . thinking.

You're nuts. Chayo, ven a saludar. *All the relatives are here. You come out of there and be sociable.*

Do boys think, and girls daydream? Do only girls have to come out and greet the relatives and smile and be nice and *quedar bien*?

It's not good to spend so much time alone.

What she do in there all by herself? It don't look right.

Chayito, when you getting married? Look at your cousin Leticia. She's younger than you.

How many kids you want when you grow up?

When I become a mommy . . .

You'll change. You'll see. Wait till you meet Mr. Right.

Chayo, tell everybody what it is you're studying again.

Look at our Chayito. She likes making her little pictures. She's gonna be a painter.

A painter! Tell her I got five rooms that need painting.

When you become a mother . . .

• • •

Thank you for making all those months I held my breath not a child in my belly, but a thyroid problem in my throat.

I can't be a mother. Not now. Maybe never. Not for me to choose, like I didn't choose being female. Like I didn't choose being artist—it isn't something you choose. It's something you are, only I can't explain it.

I don't want to be a mother.

I wouldn't mind being a father. At least a father could still be artist, could love some*thing* instead of some*one*, and no one would call that selfish.

I leave my braid here and thank you for believing what I do is important. Though no one else in my family, no other woman, neither friend nor relative, no one I know, not even the heroine in the *telenovelas*, no woman wants to live alone.

I do.

Virgencita de Guadalupe. For a long time I wouldn't let you in my house. I couldn't see you without seeing my ma each time my father came home drunk and yelling, blaming everything that ever went wrong in his life on her.

I couldn't look at your folded hands without seeing my *abuela* mumbling, "My son, my son, my son . . ." Couldn't look at you without blaming you for all the pain my mother and her mother and all our mothers' mothers have put up with in the name of God. Couldn't let you in my house.

I wanted you bare-breasted, snakes in your hands. I wanted you leaping and somersaulting the backs of bulls. I wanted you swallowing raw hearts and rattling volcanic ash. I wasn't going to be my mother or my grandma. All that self-sacrifice, all that silent suffering. Hell no. Not here. Not me.

Don't think it was easy going without you. Don't think I didn't get my share of it from everyone. Heretic. Atheist. *Malinchista. Hocicona.* But I wouldn't shut my yap. My mouth always getting me in trouble. *Is* that *what they teach you at the university? Miss High-and-Mighty. Miss Thinks-She's-Too-Good-for-Us.* Acting like a *bolilla,* a white girl. *Malinche.* Don't think it didn't hurt being called a traitor. Trying to explain to my ma, to my *abuela,* why I didn't want to be like them.

I don't know how it all fell in place. How I finally understood who you are. No longer Mary the mild, but our mother Tonantzín. Your church at Tepeyac built on the site of her temple. Sacred ground no matter whose goddess claims it.

That you could have the power to rally a people when a country was born, and again during civil war, and during a farmworkers' strike in California made me think maybe there is power in my mother's patience, strength in my grandmother's endurance. Because those who suffer have a special power, don't they? The power of understanding someone else's pain. And understanding is the beginning of healing.

When I learned your real name is Coatlaxopeuh, She Who Has Dominion over Serpents, when I recognized you as Tonantzín, and learned your names are Teteoinnan, Toci, Xochiquetzal, Tlazolteotl, Coatlicue, Chalchiuhtlicue, Coyolxauhqui, Huixtocihuatl, Chicomecoatl, Cihuacoatl, when I could see you as Nuestra Señora de la Soledad, Nuestra Señora de los Remedios, Nuestra Señora del Perpetuo Socorro, Nuestra Señora de San Juan de los Lagos, Our Lady of Lourdes, Our Lady of Mount Carmel, Our Lady of the Rosary, Our Lady of Sorrows, I wasn't ashamed, then, to be my mother's daughter, my grandmother's granddaughter, my ancestors' child.

When I could see you in all your facets, all at once the Buddha, the Tao, the true Messiah, Yahweh, Allah, the Heart of the Sky, the Heart of the Earth, the Lord of the Near and Far, the Spirit, the Light, the Universe, I could love you, and, finally, learn to love me.

Mighty Guadalupana Coatlaxopeuh Tonantzín,

What "little miracle" could I pin here? Braid of hair in its place and know that I thank you.

Rosario (Chayo) De Leon
Austin, Tejas

Los Boxers

Whoops! There goes your soda water. See. Now look. Mama, come get your little one. Watch her now, she's barefoot and could cut herself. Guess you get to mop it up, huh? I haven't dropped anything in a long time. Since I was a kid, I guess. I can't remember the last time I dropped a soda water. Big Red sure is sticky, ain't it? Gets in the clothes and don't wash out, and leaves the kids' mouths painted like clowns, right? She sure is pretty. You betcha. But oh kids, they's cute when they're little, but by the time they start turning ugly, it's too late, you already love them.

Got to watch not to buy them soda water in a glass bottle next time. Specially not Big Red. But that's the one they keep asking for the most, right? You betcha you can have my basket. My stuff ain't ready yet.

When my wife died I used to go to a place over on Calaveras way bigger than this. This ain't nothing. That place had twice as many machines. And they had dryers that was fifteen minutes for a quarter, so you didn't have to waste an extra quarter for say polyester that dries real quick. There was only two of them, though—you had to be sharp and grab 'em soon as they was free.

Here everything's thirty minutes for fifty cents. 'Spensive when you got to keep dropping quarters and quarters and quarters. Sometimes if you're lucky you could maybe get a machine that's got time on it, see. Throw in the light stuff that dries like that. Socks, washcloths, the fifty-fifty shirts maybe so they don't get wrinkled, right?

My jeans could use more than thirty minutes, though. Thirty minutes ain't enough, but I'd rather take them home damp and hang them on the windowsill before I drop in another fifty cents. It's 'cause I dry them on low, see. Before I used to dry them on high, and they'd always fit me tight later on. Lady at the K mart said, You gotta dry your jeans on low, otherwise they shrink on you. She's right. I always set them on low now, see, even though it takes longer and they're still damp after thirty minutes. Least they fit right. I learned that much.

You know what else? When you wash, it ain't enough to separate the clothes by temperature. You need to separate them by weight. Towels with towels. Jeans with jeans. Sheets with sheets. And always make sure you use plenty of water. That's the secret. Even if it's just a few things in the machine. Lots of water, got it? So's the clothes all wash better and don't take any wear and tear, see, and last longer. That's another trick I picked up too.

Make sure you don't let those clothes sit in that dryer now. You're welcome. Gotta keep on top of them, right? Soon as they stop spinning, get 'em out of there. Otherwise it just means more work later.

My T-shirts get wrinkled even if I dry them fifteen minutes hot or cold. That's T-shirts for you. Always get a little wrinkled one way or another. They's funny, T-shirts.

You know how to keep a stain from setting? Guess. Ice cube.

Yup. My wife taught me that one. I used to think she was crazy. Anytime I spilled something on the tablecloth, off she'd go running to the ice box. Spot my shirts with *mole,* ice cube. Stain a towel with blood, ice cube. Kick over a beer on the living-room rug, you got it, ice cube.

Oh boy, she was clean. Everything in the house looked new even though it was old. Towels, sheets, embroidered pillowcases, and them little table runners like doilies, them you put on chairs for your head, those, she had them white and stiff like the collar of a nun. You betcha. Starched and ironed everything. My socks, my T-shirts. Even ironed *los* boxers. Yup, drove me crazy with her ice cubes. But now that she's dead, well, that's just how life is.

There Was a Man, There Was a Woman

There was a man and there was a woman. Every payday, every other Friday, the man went to the Friendly Spot Bar to drink and spend his money. Every payday, every other Friday, the woman went to the Friendly Spot Bar to drink and spend her money. The man was paid on the second and fourth Friday of the month. The woman was paid on the first and third Friday. Because of this the man and the woman did not know each other.

The man drank and drank with his friends and believed if he drank and drank, the words for what he was feeling would slip out more readily, but usually he simply drank and said nothing. The woman drank and drank with her friends and believed if she drank and drank, the words for what she was feeling would slip out more readily, but usually she simply drank and said nothing. Every other Friday the man drank his beer and laughed loudly. Every Friday in between the woman drank her beer and laughed loudly.

At home when the night came down and the moon appeared, the woman raised her pale eyes to the moon and cried. The man in his bed contemplated the same moon, and thought about the millions who had looked at the moon before him, those who had worshiped or loved or died before that same moon, mute and lovely. Now blue light streamed inside his window and tangled itself with the glow of the sheets. The moon, the same round *O*. The man looked and swallowed.

Tin Tan Tan

Me abandonaste, mujer, porque soy muy pobre
Y por tener la desgracia de ser casado.
Que voy hacer si yo soy el abandonado,
Abandonado sea por el amor de Dios.

—"El Abandonado"

Little thorn in my soul, pebble in my shoe, jewel of my life, the passionate doll who has torn my heart in two, tell me, cruel beauty that I adore, why you torment me. I have the misfortune of being both poor and without your affection. When the hope of your caresses flowered in my soul, happiness blossomed in my tomorrows. But now that you have yanked my golden dreams from me, I shiver from this chalice of pain like a tender white flower tossed in rain. Return my life to me, and end this absurd pain. If not, Rogelio Velasco will have loved in vain.

Until death do us part, said your eyes, but not your heart. All, all illusion. A caprice of your flirtatious woman's soul. I confess I am lost between anguish and forgetting. And now if I dissolve my tears in dissipation, know, my queen, only you are to blame. My fragile heart will never be the same.

Providence knew what was in store, the day I arrived innocently at your door. Dressed in my uniform and carrying the tools of my trade, without knowing destiny waited for me, I knocked. You opened your arms, my heaven, but kept your precious heart locked.

If God wills it, perhaps these words of sentiment will convince you. Perhaps I can exterminate the pests of doubt that infest your house. Perhaps the pure love I had to offer wasn't enough, and another now is savoring your honeyed nectar. But none will love you so honorably and true as the way Rogelio Velasco loved you.

They say of the poet and madman we all have a little. Even my life I would give for your exquisite treasures. But poor me. Though others may lure you with jewels and riches, all I can offer is this humble measure.

Alone, all alone in the world, sad and small like a nightingale serenading the infinite. How could a love so tender and sweet become the cross of my pain? No, no, I can't conceive I won't receive your precious lips again. My eyes are tired of weeping, my heart of beating. If perhaps some crystal moment before dawn or twilight you remember me, bring only a bouquet of tears to lay upon my thirsty grave.

Tan TÁN

Bien Pretty

Ya me voy,
ay te dejo en San Antonio.
—Flaco Jiménez

He wasn't pretty unless you were in love with him. Then any time you met anyone with those same monkey eyes, that burnt-sugar skin, the face wider than it was long, well, you were in for it.

His family came from Michoacán. All *chaparritos,* every one of them—short even by Mexican standards—but to me he was perfect.

I'm to blame. Flavio Munguía was just ordinary Flavio until he met me. I filled up his head with a million and one *cariñitos.* Then he was ruined forever. Walked different. Looked people in the eye when he talked. Ran his eyes across every pair of *nalgas* and *chichis* he saw. I am sorry.

Once you tell a man he's pretty, there's no taking it back. They think they're pretty all the time, and I suppose, in a way, they are. It's got to do with believing it. Just the way I used to believe I was pretty. Before Flavio Munguía wore all my prettiness away.

Don't think I haven't noticed my girlfriends back home who got the good-lookers. They all look twice their age now, old from all the *corajes* exploding inside their hearts and bellies.

Because a pretty man is like a too-fancy car or a real good stereo or a microwave oven. Late or early, sooner or later, you're just asking for it. Know what I mean?

Flavio. He wrote poems and signed them "Rogelio Velasco." And maybe I would still be in love with him if he wasn't already married to two women, one in Tampico and the other in Matamoros. Well, that's what they say.

Who knows why the universe singled me out. Lupe Arredondo, stupid art thou amongst all women. Once I was as solid as a sailor on her sea legs, the days rolling steadily beneath me, and then—Flavio Munguía arrived.

Flavio entered my life via a pink circular rolled into a tube and wedged in the front gate curlicue:

$ SPECIAL $
PROMOTION
LA CUCARACHA APACHURRADA PEST CONTROL
OVER 10 YEARS OF EXPERIENCE

If you are Tired of ROACHES and Hate them like many People do, but can't afford to pay alot of Money $$$$ to have a house Free of ROACHES ROACHES ROACHES!!! We will treat your kitchen, behind and under your refrigerator and stove, inside your cabinets and even exterminate your living room all for only $20.00. Don't be fooled by the price. Call now. 555–2049 or Beeper #555–5912. We also kill spiders, beetles, scorpions, ants, fleas, and many more insects.

!!So Don't Hesitate Call Us Now!!
You'll be glad you did call us, Thank you very much.
Your CUCARACHAS will be DEAD
(*$5.00 extra for each additional room)

A dead cockroach lying on its back followed as illustration.

It's because of the river and the palm and pecan trees and the humidity and all that we have so many palmetto bugs, roaches so big they look Pleistocene. I'd never seen anything like them before. We don't have bugs like that in California, at least not in the Bay. But like they say, everything's bigger and better in Texas, and that holds especially true for bugs.

So I live near the river in one of those houses with wood floors varnished the color of Coca-Cola. It isn't mine. It belongs to Irasema Izaura Coronado, a famous Texas poet who carries herself as if she is directly descended from Ixtaccíhuatl or something. Her husband is an honest-to-God Huichol *curandero,* and she's no slouch either, with a Ph.D. from the Sorbonne.

A Fulbright whisked them to Nayarit for a year, and that's how I got to live here in the turquoise house on East Guenther, not exactly in the heart of the historic King William district—it's on the wrong side of South Alamo to qualify, the side where the peasantry lives—but close enough to the royal mansions that attract every hour on the hour the Pepto Bismol–pink tourist buses wearing sombreros.

I called La Cucaracha Apachurrada Pest Control the first month I house-sat Her Highness's home. I was sharing residence with:

(8) Oaxacan black pottery pieces
signed Diego Rivera monotype
upright piano
star-shaped piñata
(5) strings of red chile lights
antique Spanish shawl
St. Jacques Majeur Haitian voodoo banner
cappuccino maker
lemonwood Olinalá table
replica of the goddess Coatlicue
life-size papier-mâché skeleton signed by the Linares family
Frida Kahlo altar
punched tin Virgen de Guadalupe chandelier
bent-twig couch with Mexican sarape
cushions

seventeenth-century Spanish *retablo*
tree-of-life candlestick
Santa Fe plate rack
(2) identical sets of vintage Talavera Mexican dishware
eye-of-God crucifix
knotty pine armoire
pie safe
death mask of Pancho Villa with mouth slightly open
Texana chair upholstered in cowskin with longhorn horns for the arms and legs
(7) Afghan throw rugs
iron bed with a mosquito net canopy

Beneath this veneer of Southwest funk, of lace and silk and porcelain, beyond the embroidered pillows that said DUERME, MI AMOR, the Egyptian cotton sheets and eyelet bedspread, the sigh of air that barely set the gauze bedroom curtains trembling, the blue garden, the pink hydrangea, the gilt-edged tea set, the abalone-handled silver, the obsidian hair combs, the sticky, cough-medicine-and-powdered-sugar scent of magnolia blossoms, there were, as well, the roaches.

I was afraid to open drawers. I never went into the kitchen after dark. They were the same Coca-Cola color as the floors, hard to spot unless they gave themselves away in panic.

The worst thing about them wasn't their size, nor the crunch they gave under a shoe, nor the yellow grease that oozed from their guts, nor the thin shells they shed translucent as popcorn hulls, nor the possibility they might be winged and fly into your hair, no.

What made them unbearable was this. The scuttling in the middle of the night. An ugly clubfoot grate like a dead thing being dragged across the floor, a louder-than-life munching during their cannibal rites, a nervous pitter, and then patter when they scurried across the Irish-linen table runners, leaving a trail of black droppings like coffee grounds, sticky feet rustling across the clean stack of typewriter paper in the desk drawer, my primed canvasses, the set of Wedgewood rose teacups, the lace Victorian wedding dress hanging on the bedroom wall, the dried baby's breath, the white wicker vanity, the cutwork pillowcases, your blue raven hair scented with Tres Flores brilliantine.

Flavio, it's true. The house charms me now as it did then. The folk art, the tangerine-colored walls, the *urracas* at sunset. But what would you have done if you were me? I'd driven all the way from northern California to central Texas with my past pared down to what could fit inside a van. A futon. A stainless-steel wok. My grandmother's *molcajete*. A pair of flamenco shoes with crooked heels. Eleven *huipiles*. Two *rebozos—de bolita y de seda*. My Tae Kwon Do uniform. My crystals and copal. A portable boom box and all my Latin tapes—Rubén Blades, Astor Piazzolla, Gipsy Kings, Inti Illimani, Violeta Parra, Mercedes Sosa, Agustín Lara, Trio Los Panchos, Pedro Infante, Lydia Mendoza, Paco de Lucía, Lola Beltrán, Silvio Rodríguez, Celia Cruz, Juan Peña "El Lebrijano," Los Lobos, Lucha Villa, Dr. Loco and his Original Corrido Boogie Band.

Sure, I knew I was heading for trouble the day I agreed to come to Texas. But not even the *I Ching* warned me what I was in for when Flavio Munguía drove up in the pest-control van.

"*TEX*-as! *What* are you going to do *there?*" Beatriz Soliz asked this, a criminal lawyer by day, an Aztec dance instructor by night, and my closest *comadre* in all the world. Beatriz and I go back a long way. Back to the grape-boycott demonstrations in front of the Berkeley Safeway. And I mean the *first* grape strike.

"I thought I'd give Texas a year maybe. At least that. It can't be *that* bad."

"A year!!! Lupe, are you crazy? They still lynch Meskins down there. Everybody's got chain saws and gun racks and pickups and Confederate flags. *Aren't* you *scared?*"

"Girlfriend, you watch too many John Wayne movies."

To tell the truth, *Texas did* scare the hell out of me. All I knew about Texas was it was *big*. It was *hot*. And it was *bad*. Added to this was my mama's term *teja-NO-te* for *tejano,* which is sort of like "Texcessive," in a redneck kind of way. "It was one of those *teja-NO-tes* that started it," Mama would say. "You know how they are. Always looking for a fight."

I'd said yes to an art director's job at a community cultural center in San Antonio. Eduardo and I had split. For good. *C'est finis*. End of the road, buddy. *Adiós y suerte*. San Francisco is too small a town to go around dragging your three-legged heart. Café Pícaro was off limits because it was Eddie's favorite. I stopped frequenting the Café Bohème too. Missed several good openings at La Galería. Not because I was afraid of running into Eddie, but because I was terrified of confronting "*la otra*." My nemesis, in other words. A financial consultant for Merrill Lynch. A blonde.

Eddie, who I'd supported with waitress jobs that summer we were both struggling to pay our college loans *and* the rent on that tiny apartment on Balmy—big enough when we were in love, but too small when love was scarce. Eddie, who I met the year before I started teaching at the community college, the year after he gave up community organizing and worked part-time as a paralegal. Eddie, who taught me how to salsa, who lectured me night and day about human rights in Guatemala, El Salvador, Chile, Argentina, South Africa, but never said a word about the rights of Blacks in Oakland, the kids of the Tenderloin, the women who shared his bed. Eduardo. My Eddie. *That* Eddie. With a blonde. He didn't even have the decency to pick a woman of color.

A month hadn't passed since I unpacked the van, but I'd already convinced myself San Antonio was a mistake. I couldn't understand how any Spanish priest in his right mind decided to sit right down in the middle of nowhere and build a mission with no large body of water for miles. I'd always lived near the ocean. I felt landlocked and dusty. Light so white it left me dizzy, sun bleached as an onion.

In the Bay, whenever I got depressed, I always drove out to Ocean Beach. Just to sit. And, I don't know, something about looking at water, how it just goes and goes and goes, something about that I found very soothing. As if somehow I were connected to every ripple that was sending itself out and out until it reached another shore.

But I hadn't found anything to replace it in San Antonio. I wondered what San Antonians did.

I was putting in sixty-hour work weeks at the arts center. No time left to create art when I came home. I'd made a bad habit of crumpling into the couch after work, drinking half a Corona and eating a bag of Hawaiian potato chips for dinner. All the lights in the house blazing when I woke in the middle of the night, hair crooked as a broom, face creased into a mean origami, clothes wrinkled as the citizens of bus stations.

The day the pink circulars appeared, I woke up from one of these naps to find a bug crunching away on Hawaiian chips and another pickled inside my beer bottle. I called La Cucaracha Apachurrada the next morning.

So while you are spraying baseboards, the hose hissing, the gold pump clicking, bending into cupboards, reaching under sinks, the leather utility belt slung loose around your hips, I'm thinking. Thinking you might be the perfect Prince Popo for a painting I've had kicking around in my brain.

I'd always wanted to do an updated version of the Prince Popocatépetl/Princess Ixtaccíhuatl volcano myth, that tragic love story metamorphosized from classic to kitsch calendar art, like the ones you get at Carnicería Ximénez or Tortillería la Guadalupanita. Prince Popo, half-naked Indian warrior built like Johnny Weissmuller, crouched in grief beside his sleeping princess Ixtaccíhuatl, buxom as an Indian Jayne Mansfield. And behind them, echoing their silhouettes, their namesake volcanoes.

Hell, I could do better than that. It'd be fun. And you might be just the Prince Popo I've been waiting for with that face of a sleeping Olmec, the heavy Oriental eyes, the thick lips and wide nose, that profile carved from onyx. The more I think about it, the more I like the idea.

"Would you like to work for me as a model?"

"Excuse?"

"I mean I'm an artist. I need models. Sometimes. To model, you know. For a painting. I thought. You would be good. Because you have such a wonderful. Face."

Flavio laughed. I laughed too. We both laughed. We laughed and then we laughed some more. And when we were through with our laughing, he packed up his ant traps, spray tank, steel wool, clicked and latched and locked trays, toolboxes, slammed van doors shut. Laughed and drove away.

There is everything *but* a washer and dryer at the house on East Guenther. So every Sunday morning, I stuff all my dirty clothes into pillowcases and haul them out to the van, then drive over to the Kwik Wash on South Presa. I don't mind it, really. I almost like it, because across the street is Torres Taco Haven, "This Is Taco Country." I can load up five washers at a time if I get up early enough, go have a coffee and a Haven Taco—potatoes, chile, and cheese. Then a little later, throw everything in the dryer, and go back for a second cup of coffee and a Torres Special—bean, cheese, guacamole, and bacon, flour tortilla, please.

But one morning, in between the wash and dry cycles, while I ran out to reload the machines, someone had bogarted my table, the window booth next to the jukebox. I was about to get mad and say so, until I realized it was the Prince.

"Remember me? Six eighteen on Guenther."

He looked as if he couldn't remember what he was supposed to remember—then laughed that laugh, like blackbirds startled from the corn.

"Still a good joke, but I was serious. I really am a painter."

"And in reality I am a poet," he said. "*De poeta y loco todos tenemos un poco, ¿no?* But if you asked my mother she would say I'm more *loco* than *poeta*. Unfortunately, poetry only nourishes the heart and not the belly, so I work with my uncle as a bug assassin."

"Can I sit?"

"Please, please."

I ordered my second coffee and a Torres Special. A wide silence.

"What's your favorite course?"

"Art History."

"Nono nono nono nono NO," he said the way they do in Mexico—all the no's overflowing quickly quickly quickly like a fountain of champagne glasses. "*Horse,* not *course,*" and whinnied.

"Oh—horse. I don't know. Mr. Ed?" Stupid. I didn't know any horses. But Flavio smiled anyway the way he always would when I talked, as if admiring my teeth. "So. What. Will you model? Yes? I'd pay you, of course."

"Do I have to take off my clothes?"

"No, no. You just sit. Or stand there, or do whatever. Just pose. I have a studio in the garage. You'll get paid just for looking like you do."

"Well, what kind of story will I have to tell if I say no?" He wrote his name for me on a paper napkin in a tight tangle of curly black letters. "This is my uncle and aunt's number I'm giving you. I live with them."

"What's your name anyway?" I said, twisting the napkin right side up.

"Flavio. Flavio Munguía Galindo," he said, "to serve you."

Flavio's family was so poor, the best they hoped for their son was a job where he would keep his hands clean. How were they to know destiny would lead Flavio north to Corpus Christi as a dishwasher at a Luby's Cafeteria.

At least it was better than the month he'd worked as a shrimper with his cousin in Port Isabel. He still couldn't look at shrimp after that. You come home with your skin and clothes stinking of shrimp, you even start to sweat shrimp, you know. Your hands a mess from the nicks and cuts that never get a chance to heal—the salt water gets in your gloves, stinging and blistering them raw. And how working in the shrimp-processing factory is even worse—snapping those damn shrimp heads all day and the conveyor belt never ending. Your hands as soggy and swollen as ever, and your head about to split with the racket of the machinery.

Field work, he'd done that too. Cabbage, potatoes, onion. Potatoes is better than cabbage, and cabbage is better than onions. Potatoes is clean work. He liked potatoes. The fields in the spring, cool and pretty in the morning, you could think of lines of poetry as you worked, think and think and think, because they're just paying for this, right?, showing me his stubby hands, not this, touching his heart.

But onions belong to dogs and the Devil. The sacks balloon behind you in the row you're working, snipping and trimming whiskers and greens, and you gotta work fast to make any money, you use very sharp shears, see, and your fingers get nicked time and time again, and how dirty it all makes you feel—the taste of onions and dust in your mouth, your eyes stinging, and the click, click, clicking of the shears in the fields and in your head long after you come home and have had two beers.

That's when Flavio remembered his mother's parting wish—A job where your fingernails are clean, *mi'jo.* At least that. And he headed to Corpus and the Luby's.

So when Flavio's Uncle Roland asked him to come to San Antonio and help him out with his exterminating business—You can learn a trade, a skill for life. Always gonna be bugs—Flavio accepted. Even if the poisons and insecticides gave him headaches, even if he had to crawl under houses and occasionally rinse his hair with a garden hose after accidentally discovering a cat's favorite litter spot, even if now and again he saw things he didn't want to see—a possum, a rat, a snake—at least that was better than scraping chicken-fried steak and mashed potatoes from plates, better than having to keep your hands all day in soapy water like a woman, only he used the word *vieja,* which is worse.

I sent a Polaroid of the Woolworth's across from the Alamo to Beatriz Soliz. A self-portrait of me having the Tuesday–Chili Dog–Fries–Coke–$2.99–Special at the snakey S-shaped lunch counter. Wrote on the back of a Don't-Mess-with-Texas postcard: HAPPY TO REPORT AM WORKING AGAIN. AS IN *REAL* WORK. NOT THE JOB THAT FEEDS MY HABIT—EATING. BUT THE THING THAT FEEDS THE SPIRIT. COME HOME RAGGEDY-ASSED, MEAN, BUT, DAMN, I'M PAINTING. EVERY OTHER SUNDAY. KICKING *NALGA* LOOKS LIKE. OR AT LEAST TRYING. *CUÍDATE*, GIRL. *ABRAZOS*, LUPE

So every other Sunday I dragged my butt out of bed and into the garage studio to try to make some worth of my life. Flavio always there before me, like if he was the one painting me.

What I liked best about working with Flavio were the stories. Sometimes while he was posing we'd have storytelling competitions. "Your Favorite Sadness." "The Ugliest Food You Ever Ate." "A Horrible Person." One that I remember was for the category "At Last—Justice." It was really his grandma's story, but he told it well.

My grandma Chavela was from here. San Antonio I mean to say. She had five husbands, and the second one was called Fito, for Filiberto. They had my Uncle Roland who at the time of this story was nine months old. They lived by the old farmers' market, over by Commerce and Santa Rosa, in a two-room apartment. My grandma said she had beautiful dishes, an antique cabinet, a small table, two chairs, a stove, a lantern, a cedar chest full of embroidered tablecloths and towels, and a three-piece bedroom set.

And so, one Sunday she felt like visiting her sister Eulalia, who lived on the other side of town. Her husband left a dollar and change on the table for her trolley, kissed her good-bye, and left. My grandma meant to take along a bag of sweets, because Eulalia was fond of Mexican candy—burnt-milk bars, pecan brittle, sugared pumpkin, glazed orange rind, and those pretty coconut squares dyed red, white, and green like the Mexican flag—so sweet you can never finish them.

So my grandma stopped at Mi Tierra Bakery. That's when she looks down the street, and who does she see but her husband kissing a woman. It looked as if their bodies were ironing each other's clothes, she said. My grandma waved at Fito. Fito waved at my grandma. Then my grandma walked back home with the baby, packed all her clothes, her set of beautiful dishes, her tablecloths and towels, and asked a neighbor to drive her to her sister Eulalia's.

Turn here. Turn there. *What street are we on?* It doesn't matter—just do as I tell you.

The next day Fito came looking for her at Eulalia's, to explain to my grandma that the woman was just an old friend, someone he hadn't seen in a while, a long long time. Three days passed and my grandma Chavela, Eulalia, and baby Roland drove off to Cheyenne, Wyoming. They stayed there fourteen years.

Fito died in 1935 of cancer of the penis. I think it was syphilis. He used to manage a baseball team. He got hit in the crotch by a fastball.

I was explaining yin and yang. How sexual harmony put one in communion with the infinite forces of nature. The earth is yin, see, female, while heaven is male and yang. And the interaction of the two constitutes the whole shebang. You can't have one without the other. Otherwise shit is out of balance. Inhaling, exhaling. Moon, sun. Fire, water. Man, woman. All complementary forces occur in pairs.

"Ah," said Flavio, "like the *mexicano* word 'sky-earth' for the world."

"Where the hell did you learn that? The *Popul Vuh*?"

"No," Flavio said flatly. "My grandma Oralia."

I said, "This is a powerful time we're living in. We have to let go of our present way of life and search for our past, remember our destinies, so to speak. Like the *I Ching* says, returning to one's roots is returning to one's destiny."

Flavio didn't say anything, just stared at his beer for what seemed a long time. "You Americans have a strange way of thinking about time," he began. Before I could object to being lumped with the northern half of America, he went on. "You think old ages end, but that's not so. It's ridiculous to think one age has overcome another. American time is running alongside the calendar of the sun, even if your world doesn't know it."

Then, to add sting to the blow, raised his beer bottle to his lips and added, "But what do I know, right? I'm just an exterminator."

Flavio said, "I don't know anything about this Tao business, but I believe love is always eternal. Even if eternity is only five minutes."

Flavio Munguía was coming for supper. I made a wonderful paella with brown rice and tofu and a pitcher of fresh sangria. Gipsy Kings were on the tape player. I wore my Lycra mini, a pair of silver cowboy boots, and a fringed shawl across my Danskin like Carmen in that film by Carlos Saura.

Over dinner I talked about how I once had my aura massaged by an Oakland *curandera,* Afro-Brazilian dance as a means of spiritual healing, where I might find good dim sum in San Antonio, and whether a white woman had any right to claim to be an Indian shamaness. Flavio talked about how Alex El Güero from work had won a Sony boom box that morning just by being the ninth caller on 107 FM K-Suave, how his Tía Tencha makes the best tripe soup ever no lie, how before leaving Corpus he and Johnny Canales from *El Show de Johnny Canales* had been like this until a bet over Los Bukis left them not speaking to each other, how every Thursday night he works out at a gym on Calaveras with aims to build himself a body better than Mil Mascara's, and is there an English equivalent for the term *la fulana*?

I served Jerez and played Astor Piazzolla. Flavio said he preferred "pure tango," classic and romantic like Gardel, not this cat-howling crap. He rolled back the Afghan rug, yanked me to my feet, demonstrated *la habanera, el fandango, la milonga,* and explained how each had contributed to birth *el tango.*

Then he ran outside to his truck, the backs of his thighs grazing my knees as he edged past me and the Olinalá coffee table. I felt all the hairs on my body sway as if I were an underwater plant and a current had set me in motion. Before I could steady myself he was popping a cassette into the tape player. A soft crackling. Then sugary notes rising like a blue satin banner held aloft by doves.

"*Violín, violonchelo, piano, salterio.* Music from the time of my *abuelos.* My grandma taught me the dances—*el chotis, cancán, los valses.* All part of that lost epoch," he said. "But that was long long ago, before the time all the dogs were named after Woodrow Wilson."

"Don't you know any indigenous dances?" I finally asked, "like *el baile de los viejitos*?"

Flavio rolled his eyes. That was the end of our dance lesson.

"Who dresses you?"

"Silver."

"What's that? A store or a horse?"

"Neither. Silver Galindo. My San Antonio cousin."

"What kind of name is Silver?"

"It's English," Flavio said, "for Silvestre."

I said, "What *you* are, sweetheart, is a product of American imperialism," and plucked at the alligator on his shirt.

I don't have to dress in a sarape and sombrero to be Mexican," Flavio said. "I *know* who *I* am."

I wanted to leap across the table, throw the Oaxacan black pottery pieces across the room, swing from the punched tin chandelier, fire a pistol at his Reeboks, and force him to dance. I wanted to *be*

Mexican at that moment, but it was true. I was not Mexican. Instead of the volley of insults I intended, all I managed to sling was a single clay pebble that dissolved on impact—*perro*. "Dog." It wasn't even the word I'd meant to hurl.

You have, how do I say it, something. Something I can't even put my finger on. Some way of moving, of not moving, that belongs to no one but Flavio Munguía. As if your body and bones always remembered you were made by a God who loved you, the one Mama talked about in her stories.

God made men by baking them in an oven, but he forgot about the first batch, and that's how Black people were born. And then he was so anxious about the next batch, he took them out of the oven too soon, so that's how White people were made. But the third batch he let cook until they were golden-golden-golden, and, honey, that's you and me.

God made you from red clay, Flavio, with his hands. This face of yours like the little clay heads they unearth in Teotihuacán. Pinched this cheekbone, then that. Used obsidian flints for the eyes, those eyes dark as the sacrificial wells they cast virgins into. Selected hair thick as cat whiskers. Thought for a long time before deciding on this nose, elegant and wide. And the mouth, ah! Everything silent and powerful and very proud kneaded into the mouth. And then he blessed you, Flavio, with skin sweet as burnt-milk candy, smooth as river water. He made you *bien* pretty even if I didn't always know it. Yes, he did.

Romelia. Forever. That's what his arm said. Forever Romelia in ink once black that had paled to blue. Romelia. Romelia. Seven thin blue letters the color of a vein. "Romelia" said his forearm where the muscle swelled into a flat stone. "Romelia" it trembled when he held me. "Romelia" by the light of the votive lamp above the bed. But when I unbuttoned his shirt a bannered cross above his left nipple murmured "Elsa."

I'd never made love in Spanish before. I mean not with anyone whose *first* language was Spanish. There was crazy Graham, the anarchist labor organizer who'd taught me to eat jalapeños and swear like a truck mechanic, but he was Welsh and had learned his Spanish running guns to Bolivia.

And Eddie, sure. But Eddie and I were products of our American education. Anything tender always came off sounding like the subtitles to a Buñuel film.

But Flavio. When Flavio accidentally hammered his thumb, he never yelled "Ouch!" he said "*¡Ay!*" The true test of a native Spanish speaker.

¡Ay! To make love in Spanish, in a manner as intricate and devout as la Alhambra. To have a lover sigh *mi vida, mi preciosa, mi chiquitita,* and whisper things in that language crooned to babies, that language murmured by grandmothers, those words that smelled like your house, like flour tortillas, and the inside of your daddy's hat, like everyone talking in the kitchen at the same time, or sleeping with the windows open, like sneaking cashews from the crumpled quarter-pound bag Mama always hid in her lingerie drawer after she went shopping with Daddy at the Sears.

That language. That sweep of palm leaves and fringed shawls. That startled fluttering, like the heart of a goldfinch or a fan. Nothing sounded dirty or hurtful or corny. How could I think of making love in English again? English with its starched *r*'s and *g*'s. English with its crisp linen syllables. English crunchy as apples, resilient and stiff as sailcloth.

But Spanish whirred like silk, rolled and puckered and hissed. I held Flavio close to me, in the mouth of my heart, inside my wrists.

Incredible happiness. A sigh unfurled of its own accord, a groan heaved out from my chest so rusty and full of dust it frightened me. I was crying. It surprised us both.

"My soul, did I hurt you?" Flavio said in that other language.

I managed to bunch my mouth into a knot and shake my head "no" just as the next wave of sobs began. Flavio rocked me, and cooed, and rocked me. *Ya, ya, ya.* There, there, there.

I wanted to say so many things, but all I could think of was a line I'd read in the letters of Georgia O'Keeffe years ago and had forgotten until then. Flavio . . . did you ever feel like flowers?

We take my van and a beer. Flavio drives. Watching Flavio's profile, that beautiful Tarascan face of his, something that ought to be set in jade. We don't have to say anything the whole ride and it's fine, just take turns sharing the one beer, back and forth, back and forth, just looking at each other from the corner of the eye, just smiling from the corner of the mouth.

What's happened to me? Flavio was just Flavio, a man I wouldn't've looked at twice before. But now anyone who reminds me of him, any baby with that same cane-sugar skin, any moon-faced woman in line at the Handy Andy, or bag boy with tight hips carrying my groceries to the car, or child at the Kwik Wash with ears as delicate as the whorls of a sea mollusk, I find myself looking at, lingering over, appreciating. Henceforth and henceforth. Forever and ever. Ad infinitum.

When I was with Eddie, we'd be making love, and then out of nowhere I would think of the black-and-white label on the tube of titanium yellow paint. Or a plastic Mickey Mouse change purse I once had with crazy hypnotized eyes that blinked open/shut, open/shut when you wobbled it. Or a little scar shaped like a mitten on the chin of a boy named Eliberto Briseño whom I was madly in love with all through the fifth grade.

But with Flavio it's just the opposite. I might be working on a charcoal sketch, chewing on a pinch of a kneaded rubber eraser I've absentmindedly put in my mouth, and then suddenly I'm thinking about the thickness of Flavio's earlobes between my teeth. Or a wisp of violet smoke might rise from someone's cigarette at the Bar America, and remind me of that twist of sinew from wrist to elbow in Flavio's pretty arms. Or say Danny and Craig from Tienda Guadalupe Folk Art & Gifts are demonstrating how South American rain sticks work, and boom—there's Flavio's voice like the pull of the ocean when it drags everything with it back to its center—that kind of gravelly, charcoal and shell and glass rasp to it. Incredible.

Taco Haven was crowded the way it always is Sunday mornings, full of grandmothers and babies in their good clothes, boys with hair still wet from the morning bath, big husbands in tight shirts, and rowdy mamas slapping rude children to public decency.

Three security guards were vacating my window booth, and we grabbed it. Flavio ordered *chilaquiles* and I ordered breakfast tacos. We asked for quarters for the jukebox, same as always. Five songs 50 cents. I punched 132, "All My Ex's Live in Texas," George Strait; 140, "Soy Infeliz," Lola Beltrán; 233, "Polvo y Olvido," Lucha Villa; 118, "Mal Hombre," Lydia Mendoza; and number 167, "La Movidita," because I knew Flavio loved Flaco Jiménez.

Flavio was no more quiet than usual, but midway through breakfast he announced, "My life, I have to go."

"We just got here."

"No. I mean me. *I* must go. To Mexico."

"What are you talking about?"

"My mother wrote me. I have compromises to attend to."

"But you're coming back. Right?"

"Only destiny knows."

A red dog with stiff fur tottered by the curb.

"What are you trying to tell me?"

The same red color as a cocoa doormat or those wooden-handled scrub brushes you buy at the Winn's.

"I mean I have family obligations." There was a long pause.

You could tell the dog was real sick. Big bald patches. Gummy eyes that bled like grapes.

"My mother writes that my sons—"

"Sons . . . How many?"

"Four. From my first. Three from my second."

"First. Second. What? Marriages?"

"No, only one marriage. The other doesn't count since we weren't married in a church."

"Christomatic."

Really it made you sick to look at the thing, hobbling about like that in jerky steps as if it were dancing backward and had only three legs.

"But this has nothing to do with you, Lupe. Look, you love your mother *and* your father, don't you?"

The dog was eating something, jaws working in spasmodic gulps. A bean-and-cheese taco, I think.

"Loving one person doesn't take away from loving another. It's that way with me with love. One has nothing to do with the other. In all seriousness and with all my heart I tell you this, Lupe."

Somebody must've felt sorry for it and tossed it a last meal, but the kind thing would've been to shoot it.

"So that's how it is."

"There is no other remedy. *La* yin *y el* yang, you know," Flavio said and meant it.

"Well, yeah," I said. And then because my Torres Special felt like it wanted to rise from my belly—"I think you better go now. I gotta get my clothes out of the dryer before they get wrinkled."

"*Es* cool," Flavio said, sliding out of the booth and my life. "*Ay te wacho,* I guess."

I looked for my rose-quartz crystal and visualized healing energy surrounding me. I lit copal and burned sage to purify the house. I put on a tape of Amazon flutes, Tibetan gongs, and Aztec ocarinas, tried to center on my seven chakras, and thought only positive thoughts, expressions of love, compassion, forgiveness. But after forty minutes I still had an uncontrollable desire to drive over to Flavio Munguía's house with my grandmother's *molcajete* and bash in his skull.

What kills me is your silence. So certain, so solid. Not a note, nor postcard. Not a phone call, no number I could reach you at. No address I could write to. Neither yes nor no.

Just the void. The days raw and wide as this drought-blue sky. Just this nothingness. That's what hurts.

Nothing wants to break from the eyes. When you're a kid, it's easy. You take one wooden step out in the hall dark and wait. The hallways of every house we ever lived in smelling of Pine-Sol and dirty-looking no matter how many Saturdays we scrubbed it. Chipped paint and ugly nicks and craters in the walls from a century of bikes and kids' shoes and downstairs tenants. The handrail old and never beautiful, not even the day it was new, I bet. Darkness soaked in the plaster and wood when the house was divided into apartments. Dust balls and hair in the corners where the broom didn't reach. And now and then, a mouse squeaking.

How I let the sounds, dark and full of dust and hairs, out of my throat and eyes, that sound mixed with spit and coughing and hiccups and bubbles of snot. And the sea trickling out of my eyes as if I'd always carried it inside me, like a seashell waiting to be cupped to an ear.

These days we run from the sun. Cross the street quick, get under an awning. Carry an umbrella like tightrope walkers. Red-white-and-blue-flowered nylon. Beige with green and red stripes. Faded maroon with an amber handle. Bus ladies slouched and fanning themselves with a newspaper and a bandanna.

Bad news. The sky is blue again today and will be blue again tomorrow. Herd of clouds big as longhorns passing mighty and grazing low. Heat like a husband asleep beside you, like someone breathing in your ear who you just want to shove once, good and hard, and say, "Quit it."

When I was doing collages, I bought a few "powders" from Casa Preciado Religious Articles, the Mexican voodoo shop on South Laredo. I remember I'd picked Te Tengo Amarrado y Claveteado and Regresa a Mí—just for the wrapper. But I found myself hunting around for them this morning, and when I couldn't find them, making a special trip back to that store that smells of chamomile and black bananas.

The votive candles are arranged like so. Church-sanctioned powers on one aisle—San Martín de Porres, Santo Niño de Atocha, el

Sagrado Corazón, La Divina Providencia, Nuestra Señora de San Juan de los Lagos. Folk powers on another—El Gran General Pancho Villa, Ajo Macho/Garlic Macho, La Santísima Muerte/Blessed Death, Bingo Luck, Law Stay Away, Court Case Double Strength. Back to back, so as not to offend maybe. I chose a Yo Puedo Más Que Tú from the pagan side and a Virgen de Guadalupe from the Christian.

Magic oils, magic perfume and soaps, votive candles, *milagritos,* holy cards, magnet car-statuettes, plaster saints with eyelashes made from human hair, San Martín Caballero good-luck horseshoes, incense and copal, aloe vera bunched, blessed, bound with red string, and pinned above a door. Herbs stocked from floor to ceiling in labeled drawers.

AGUACATE, ALBAHACA, ALTAMISA, ANACAHUITE, BARBAS DE ELOTE, CEDRÓN DE CASTILLO, COYOTE, CHARRASQUILLA, CHOCOLATE DE INDIO, EUCALIPTO, FLOR DE ACOCOTILLO, FLOR DE AZAHAR, FLOR DE MIMBRE, FLOR DE TILA, FLOR DE ZEMPOAL, HIERBABUENA, HORMIGA, HUISACHE, MANZANILLA, MARRUBIO, MIRTO, NOGAL, PALO AZUL, PASMO, PATA DE VACA, PIONÍA, PIRUL, RATÓN, TEPOZÁN, VÍBORA, ZAPOTE BLANCO, ZARZAMORA.

Snake, rat, ant, coyote, cow hoof. Were there actually dead animals tucked in a drawer? A skin wrapped in tissue paper, a dried ear, a paper cone of shriveled black alphabets, a bone ground to crystals in a baby-food jar. Or were they just herbs that *looked* like the animal?

These candles and *yerbas* and stuff, do they really work? The sisters Preciado pointed to a sign above their altar to Our Lady of the Remedies. *VENDEMOS, NO HACEMOS RECETAS.* WE SELL, WE DON'T PRESCRIBE.

I can be brave in the day, but nights are my Gethsemane. That pinch of the dog's teeth just as it nips. A mean South American itch somewhere I can't reach. The little hurricane of bathwater just before it slips inside the drain.

Seems like the world is spinning smooth without a bump or squeak except when love comes in. Then the whole machine just quits like a loud load of wash on imbalance—the buzzer singing to high heaven, the danger light flashing.

Not true. The world has always turned with its trail of tin cans rattling behind it. I have always been in love with a man.

Everything's like it was. Except for this. When I look in the mirror, I'm ugly. How come I never noticed before?

I was having *sopa tarasca* at El Mirador and reading Dear Abby. A letter from "Too Late," who wrote now that his father was dead, he was sorry he had never asked his forgiveness for having hurt him, he'd never told his father "I love you."

I pushed my bowl of soup away and blew my nose with my paper napkin. *I'd* never asked Flavio forgiveness for having hurt him. And yes, I'd never said "I love you." I'd never said it, though the words rattled in my head like *urracas* in the bamboo.

For weeks I lived with those two regrets like twin grains of sand embedded in my oyster heart, until one night listening to Carlos Gardel sing, "*Life is an absurd wound,*" I realized I had it wrong. oh.

Today the Weber kettle in the backyard finally quit. Three days of thin white smoke like kite string. I'd stuffed in all of Flavio's letters and poems and photos and cards and all the sketches and studies I'd ever done of him, then lit a match. I didn't expect paper to take so long to burn, but it was a lot of layers. I had to keep poking it with a stick. I did save one poem, the last one he gave me before he left. Pretty in Spanish. But you'll have to take my word for it. In English it just sounds goofy.

The smell of paint was giving me headaches. I couldn't bring myself to look at my canvasses. I'd turn on the TV. The Galavisión channel. Told myself I was looking for old Mexican movies. María Félix, Jorge Negrete, Pedro Infante, anything, please, where somebody's singing on a horse.

After a few days I'm watching the *telenovelas*. Avoiding board meetings, rushing home from work, stopping at Torres Taco Haven on the way and buying taquitos to go. Just so I could be seated in front of the screen in time to catch *Rosa Salvaje* with Verónica Castro as the savage Rose of the title. Or Daniela Romo in *Balada por un Amor*. Or Adela Noriega in *Dulce Desafío*. I watched them all. In the name of research.

I started dreaming of these Rosas and Briandas and Luceros. And in my dreams I'm slapping the heroine to her senses, because I want them to be women who make things happen, not women who things happen to. Not loves that are *tormentosos*. Not men powerful and passionate versus women either volatile and evil, or sweet and resigned. But women. Real women. The ones I've loved all my life. *If you don't like it* lárgate, *honey*. Those women. The ones I've known everywhere except on TV, in books and magazines. *Las* girlfriends. *Las comadres*. Our mamas and *tías*. Passionate *and* powerful, tender and volatile, brave. And, above all, fierce.

"*Bien* pretty, your shawl. You didn't buy it in San Antonio?" Centeno's Mexican Supermarket. The cashier was talking to me.

"No, it's Peruvian. Think I bought it in Santa Fe. Or New York. I don't remember."

"*Que* cute. You look real *mona*."

Plastic hair combs with fringy flowers. Purple blouse crocheted out of shiny yarn, not tucked but worn over her jeans to hide a big stomach. I know—I do the same thing.

She's my age, but looks old. Tired. Never mind the red lips, the eye makeup that just makes her look sad. Those creases from the corner of the lip to the wing of the nostril from holding in anger, or tears. Or both. She's the one ringing up my *Vanidades*. "Extraordinary Issue." "Julio Confesses He's Looking for Love." "Still Daddy's Girl?—Liberate Yourself!" "15 Ways to Say I Love You with Your Eyes." "The Incredible Wedding of Argentine Soccer Star Maradona (It Cost 3 Million U.S. Dollars!)" "*Summer by the Sea*, a Complete Novel by Corín Tellado."

"Libertad Palomares," she said, looking at the cover.

"*Amar es Vivir*," I answered automatically as if it were my motto. Libertad Palomares. A big Venezuelan *telenovela* star. Big on crying. Every episode she weeps like a Magdalene. Not me. I couldn't cry if my life depended on it.

"Right she works her part real good?"

"I never miss an episode." That was the truth.

"Me neither. *Si Dios quiere* I'm going to get home in time today to watch it. It's getting good."

"Looks like it's going to finish pretty soon."

"Hope not. How much is this? I might buy one too. *Three-fifty! Bien* 'spensive."

Maybe once. Or maybe never. Maybe each time someone asks, *Wanna dance?* at Club Fandango. All for a Saturday night at Hacienda Salas Party House on South Mission Road. Or Lerma's Night Spot on Zarzamora. Making eyes at Ricky's Poco Loco Club or El

Taconazo Lounge. Or maybe, like in my case, in my garage making art.

Amar es Vivir. What it comes down to for that woman at Centeno's and for me. It was enough to keep us tuning in every day at six-thirty, another episode, another thrill. To relive that living when the universe ran through the blood like river water. Alive. Not the weeks spent writing grant proposals, not the forty hours standing behind a cash register shoving cans of refried beans into plastic sacks. Hell, no. This wasn't what we were put on the planet for. Not ever.

Not Lola Beltrán sobbing "*Soy infeliz*" into her four *cervezas*. But Daniela Romo singing "*Ya no. Es verdad que te adoro, pero más me adoro yo.*" I love you, honey, but I love me more.

One way or another. Even if it's only the lyrics to a stupid pop hit. We're going to right the world and live. I mean live our lives the way lives were meant to be lived. With the throat and wrists. With rage and desire, and joy and grief, and love till it hurts, maybe. But goddamn, girl. Live.

Went back to the twin volcano painting. Got a good idea and redid the whole thing. Prince Popo and Princess Ixta trade places. After all, who's to say the sleeping mountain isn't the prince, and the voyeur the princess, right? So I've done it my way. With Prince Popocatépetl lying on his back instead of the Princess. Of course, I had to make some anatomical adjustments in order to simulate the geographical silhouettes. I think I'm going to call it *El Pipi del Popo*. I kind of like it.

Everywhere I go, it's me and me. Half of me living my life, the other half watching me live it. Here it is January already. Sky wide as an ocean, shark-belly gray for days at a time, then all at once a blue so tender you can't remember how only months before the heat split you open like a pecan shell, you can't remember anything anymore.

Every sunset, I find myself rushing, cleaning the brushes, hurrying, my footsteps giving a light tap on each rung up the aluminum ladder to the garage roof.

Because *urracas* are arriving by the thousands from all directions and settling in the river trees. Trees leafless as sea anemones in this season, the birds in their branches dark and distinct as treble clefs, very crisp and noble and clean as if someone had cut them out of black paper with sharp scissors and glued them with library paste.

Urracas. Grackles. *Urracas*. Different ways of looking at the same bird. City calls them grackles, but I prefer *urracas*. That roll of the *r* making all the difference.

Urracas, then, big as crows, shiny as ravens, swooping and whooping it up like drunks at Fiesta. *Urracas* giving a sharp cry, a slippery rise up the scales, a quick stroke across a violin string. And then a splintery whistle that they loop and lasso from that box in their throat, and spit and chirrup and chook. *Chook-chook, chook-chook.*

Here and there a handful of starlings tossed across the sky. All swooping in one direction. Then another explosion of starlings very far away, like pepper. Wind rattling pecans from the trees. *Thunk, thunk.* Like bad kids throwing rocks at your house. The damp smell of the earth the same smell of tea boiling.

Urracas curving, descending on treetops. Wide wings against blue. Branch tips trembling when they land, quivering when they take off again. Those at the crown devoutly facing one direction toward a private Mecca.

And other charter members off and running, high high up. Some swooping in one direction and others crisscrossing. Like marching bands at halftime. This swoop never bumping into that. *Urracas* closer to earth, starlings higher up because they're smaller. Every day. Every sunset. And no one noticing except to look at the ground and say, "Who's gonna clean up this *shit*!"

All the while the sky is throbbing. Blue, violet, peach, not holding still for one second. The sun setting and setting, all the light in the world soft as nacre, a Canaletto, an apricot, an earlobe.

And every bird in the universe chittering, jabbering, clucking, chirruping, squawking, gurgling, going crazy because God-bless-it another day has ended, as if it never had yesterday and never will again tomorrow. Just because it's today, today. With no thought of the future or past. Today. Hurray. Hurray!

¡tan ***TÁN!***

About the Author

SANDRA CISNEROS was born in Chicago in 1954. She has worked as a teacher to high school dropouts, a poet-in-the-schools, a college recruiter, and an arts administrator. Most recently, she has taught as a visiting writer at a number of universities around the country. The recipient of two NEA fellowships for poetry and fiction, as well as the Lannan Literary Award for 1991, Cisneros is the author of *Woman Hollering Creek*, *The House on Mango Street*, and *My Wicked Wicked Ways*, a volume of poetry. Her work has been translated into five languages.

The daughter of a Mexican father and a Mexican-American mother, and a sister to six brothers, she is nobody's mother and nobody's wife. She currently lives in San Antonio, Texas, where she is at work on a new novel.

ALSO BY
Sandra Cisneros

LOOSE WOMAN
Poems

"Poignant . . . lyrical, passionate . . . cool and delicate . . . hot as chili peppers." —Boston Globe

With *Loose Woman*, Sandra Cisneros gives us a vibrant collection of poems with the lilt of *Norteño* music, the ferocity of an Aztec death-goddess, and the romantic abandon of Saturday night in a border town. By turns sensual and introspective, this is a work that is at once a tour de force and a triumphant outpouring of pure soul.

"A unique feminist voice that is at once frank, saucy, realistic, audacious. Cisneros unravels her most private thoughts about love, sex, womanhood and her dual cultures." —*Time*

Poetry/0-679-75527-6

VINTAGE CONTEMPORARIES

___ **Angels** by Denis Johnson	$7.95	0-394-75987-7
___ **Fiskadoro** by Denis Johnson	$6.95	0-394-74367-9
___ **The Stars at Noon** by Denis Johnson	$5.95	0-394-75427-1
___ **Mischief Makers** by Nettie Jones	$9.00	0-679-72785-X
___ **Obscene Gestures for Women** by Janet Kauffman	$8.95	0-679-73055-9
___ **Asa, as I Knew Him** by Susanna Kaysen	$4.95	0-394-74985-5
___ **Far Afield** by Susanna Kaysen	$9.95	0-394-75822-6
___ **Lulu Incognito** by Raymond Kennedy	$7.95	0-394-75641-X
___ **Steps** by Jerzy Kosinski	$9.00	0-394-75716-5
___ **The Garden State** by Gary Krist	$7.95	0-679-72515-6
___ **House of Heroes and Other Stories** by Mary La Chapelle	$8.95	0-679-72457-5
___ **White Girls** by Lynn Lauber	$9.00	0-679-73411-2
___ **The Chosen Place, the Timeless People** by Paule Marshall	$12.95	0-394-72633-2
___ **The Beginning of Sorrows** by David Martin	$7.95	0-679-72459-1
___ **A Recent Martyr** by Valerie Martin	$7.95	0-679-72158-4
___ **The Consolation of Nature and Other Stories** by Valerie Martin	$6.95	0-679-72159-2
___ **Suttree** by Cormac McCarthy	$6.95	0-394-74145-5
___ **California Bloodstock** by Terry McDonell	$8.95	0-679-72168-1
___ **The Bushwhacked Piano** by Thomas McGuane	$8.95	0-394-72642-1
___ **Keep the Change** by Thomas McGuane	$9.95	0-679-73033-8
___ **Nobody's Angel** by Thomas McGuane	$9.95	0-394-74738-0
___ **Something to Be Desired** by Thomas McGuane	$6.95	0-394-73156-5
___ **To Skin a Cat** by Thomas McGuane	$8.95	0-394-75521-9
___ **Spider** by Patrick McGrath	$10.00	0-679-73630-1
___ **Bright Lights, Big City** by Jay McInerney	$5.95	0-394-72641-3
___ **Ransom** by Jay McInerney	$8.95	0-394-74118-8
___ **Story of My Life** by Jay McInerney	$6.95	0-679-72257-2
___ **Homeboy** by Seth Morgan	$11.00	0-679-73395-7
___ **The Beggar Maid** by Alice Munro	$10.00	0-679-73271-3
___ **Friend of My Youth** by Alice Munro	$10.00	0-679-72957-7
___ **The Moons of Jupiter** by Alice Munro	$10.00	0-679-73270-5
___ **Mama Day** by Gloria Naylor	$10.00	0-679-72181-9
___ **The All-Girl Football Team** by Lewis Nordan	$5.95	0-394-75701-7
___ **Welcome to the Arrow-Catcher Fair** by Lewis Nordan	$6.95	0-679-72164-9

Ellen Foster

by Kaye Gibbons

The story of a young girl who overcomes adversity with a combination of charm, humor, and ferocity.

"Ellen Foster is a southern Holden Caulfield, tougher perhaps, as funny...a breathtaking first novel." —Walker Percy

0-679-72886-X/$9.00

The Chosen Place, the Timeless People

by Paule Marshall

A novel set on a devastated part of a Caribbean island, whose tense relationships—between natives and foreigners, blacks and whites, haves and have-nots—keenly dramatize the vicissitudes of power.

"Unforgettable...monumental." —*Washington Post Book World*

0-394-72633-2/$13.00

Keep the Change

by Thomas McGuane

The story of Joe Starling: rancher, painter, and lover, and his struggle to right himself.

"I don't know of another writer who can walk McGuane's literary high wire. He can describe the sky, a bird, a rock, the dawn, with such grace that you want to go see for yourself; then he can zip to a scene so funny that you laugh out loud."

—*The New York Times Book Review*

0-679-73033-8/$9.95

Bright Lights, Big City

by Jay McInerney

Living in Manhattan as if he owned it, a young man tries to outstrip the approach of dawn with nothing but his wit, good will and controlled substances.

"A dazzling debut, smart, heartfelt, and very, very funny." —Tobias Wolff

0-394-72641-3/$5.95

Friend of My Youth

by Alice Munro

Ten miraculously accomplished stories that not only astonish and delight but also convey the unspoken mysteries at the heart of human experience.

"She is our Chekhov, and is going to outlast most of her contemporaries."

—Cynthia Ozick

0-679-72957-7/$10.00